THE RIGHTFUL HEIR

Maura Hagan and her companion Ellen Blacklock take rooms in a boarding house in Bath. Ellen believes their stay will help Maura to regain her strength before returning to Battle Tower in Northumberland — home of the Webber family. There, she'd suffered so much, from Basil's attempts to crush her spirit, to his cousin Herbert's malicious intentions, and love had ended in tragedy. However, in Bath she meets a man from her past who urges her to build her life anew . . .

LILLIE HOLLAND

THE RIGHTFUL HEIR

Complete and Unabridged

LINFORD
Leicester

First published in Great Britain in 1975

First Linford Edition
published 2013

A catalogue record for this book is available
from the British Library.

ISBN 978–1–4448–1574–0

Published by
F. A. Thorpe (Publishing)
Anstey, Leicestershire

Set by Words & Graphics Ltd.
Anstey, Leicestershire
Printed and bound in Great Britain by
T. J. International Ltd., Padstow, Cornwall

This book is printed on acid-free paper

To the memory of
my brother

1

'Look, Miss Maura — I bought this bonnet for you. And I've ordered two gowns to be made for you,' said Nellie eagerly. 'Try it on.'

She handed me a bonnet the colour of bluebells. 'The same as your eyes, Miss Maura.'

I looked at it. 'Yes,' I said slowly. 'Whatever happens, the colour of your eyes never changes. Everything else can change, but not that.'

I glanced in the mirror. 'My hair was golden once,' I said. 'Where did the gold go, Nellie?'

'It will come back — you see! I'll pour camomile flowers over it. Soon it will grow, and be thick and golden again.'

I studied my reflection. How pale I was — I who had once disliked the rounded pinkness of my cheeks. Well, the roundness had gone now. It was the

1

same face, but different somehow. There were little hollows under my cheekbones. Somewhat reluctantly I put on the bonnet.

'You look lovely,' cried Nellie, her face flushing with pleasure. I could feel none, though. I smiled bitterly.

'I can't wear it, anyway. I can't walk about like a normal person,' I said. 'It's no use, Nellie. I've no particular desire to go out — even if the doctor says I can.'

Nellie plumped herself down in a chair, her worn face worried.

'But you must,' she said. 'It's what I've waited for — lived for, hoped for. A new life, Miss Maura. You owe it to yourself — you owe it to me.'

Without speaking, I handed the bonnet back to her, and walked restlessly over to the window. It was raining; the elegant Georgian crescent was deserted.

'Why are we here?' I asked.

'Well, Miss Maura, I thought if we came away, to the south west first, it would give you a chance to get your strength back, before we thought about anything else. It is barely spring yet. At the end of the summer, perhaps — '

'At the end of the summer — what?'

'I thought perhaps you would be well enough to make the journey back to — back to — '

'Back to Northumberland? To Battle Tower? To live there — to live there?'

I sank down into a chair, and the weak tears began to force their way into my eyes. Nellie wrapped her arms around me, as she had so often done when I was a child.

'Don't fret yourself about it, Miss Maura. You're not strong enough yet to think about anything. Just rest yourself — I'll have some supper sent up. You'll feel better tomorrow.'

In the bedroom she helped me undress with well remembered tenderness.

With a sigh I sank back into the large feather bed, and looked round the room. Such luxury. A carpet on the

3

floor, and a washbasin and ewer with the tiniest and prettiest of roses on it. I felt that I was not entitled to it — that it was all a dream, being in pleasant rooms in Bath, with Nellie looking after me.

'Tell me it's real — that it's not a dream,' I whispered.

'You're still mixed up, Miss Maura! Of course it's not a dream. I'm here to take care of you — like I've always taken care of you. Don't tremble so — I'll give you your medicine.'

When finally I slept for the night, my rest was disturbed by the recurring nightmare which seemed to be haunting my convalescence. It was always the same; I was standing in a great, stone-flagged hall, in a lonely castle, vast and cold, peopled by unfriendly faces. The disapproving face of an elderly woman floated in front of me, her eyes hostile and gleaming. Then I seemed to see her son staring at me, desire in his eyes — desire which changed to malicious hatred.

There was another face, too, heavily moustached, calculating, with a curious, unwavering gaze that filled me with a nameless fear . . . and behind that face, another, but completely concealed under a thick, black veil; a face so terrible, so terrifying, that it was shrouded from view. As I watched, she began to remove her veil — no, I could not stand it — it was too dreadful to be borne! I screamed loudly, and woke suddenly, shaking with fright, not realizing at first that I was in a comfortable feather bed in a small but charming house in Bath.

'Miss Maura! Miss Maura!' came Nellie's gentle voice. 'It's past nine o'clock — it's morning, and you've slept well. You've been making little noises in your sleep just now, though. That nasty dream again, I suppose.'

She moved beside the bed. She had already made her toilet; as usual her hair was coiled in neat braids round her head. I could never remember seeing it done any other way. Her overwhelming goodness to me, her unchanging faithfulness and tenderness filled me with a momentary feeling of shame, almost unworthiness. I looked back over the long, terrible years which lay behind me, and knew that without her strength I would surely have perished.

'Yes, the dream again, Nellie,' I said, trying to smile.

'But look, Miss Maura, you are not there — you are here, at number thirty-five, Chippenham Crescent, Bath.'

I glanced round the room. The curtains at the window and my bed were of a rose-coloured brocade, and the carpet was a soft, moss green. The flower sprigs on the wallpaper repeated these colours. There was no doubt that two ladies spending some time in the lovely city of Bath could enjoy every comfort at Mrs Marchbanks' house.

If I were going to remain confined to these rooms day after day, though, what kind of life was that for Nellie? Did I not owe it to this gentle, patient woman to make some effort to overcome my fear of going out? Propped up in bed against the feather pillows, I considered this as I sipped my breakfast coffee.

We had travelled down from the north a month before, as soon as I was well enough to stand the journey. I had been heavily veiled; the thought of people looking at me filled me with panic. I watched Nellie thoughtfully as she carefully measured out a wineglassful of the tonic the doctor had prescribed for me. Obediently I swallowed it. It was bitter and unpleasant, but she was convinced it would do me good. She made preparations for my toilet; hot water was brought, and feeling faintly guilty at enjoying such luxury, I allowed myself to be dressed. Then Nellie brushed my hair.

'A hundred strokes, Miss Maura, that was what you had. Fifty at night, and fifty in the morning. And it shone like gold.'

'And much good it did me,' I said. Immediately I was ashamed of myself. 'You are kind, Nellie. Perhaps it will shine again — who knows?'

'It will shine again as the sun shines after too long a winter.'

For a simple, practical woman, Nellie sometimes had a surprisingly poetical turn of speech.

'Too long a winter,' I repeated. 'Yes, I think that sums it up.'

'Today I will unpack your trinkets and things — little treasures you kept from nursery days. I thought you might want them round you, to give you comfort.'

We went out of the bedroom, and into our charming sitting room. Nellie drew a chair up to the window, so that I could enjoy both the sunshine and the warmth from the fire.

I sat and looked through the long lace curtains at the sandstone houses opposite. A smart carriage was waiting outside one of them. After a while, two very elegant ladies emerged, with a young man in attendance. The younger lady was dressed in grey, with a grey squirrel cape, and a jaunty little tipped-forward hat. Evidently this was the latest fashion. The other one was resplendent in magenta. She was tall and dignified; probably the girl's mother, or perhaps an aunt. I watched the young man helping them both into the carriage. He was taking the young lady out for a drive, and the well-dressed matron was acting as chaperon, that was obvious. A strange feeling stirred inside me as I watched the coachman urge the two fine bays to a trot.

I turned my eyes away from the window. Nellie was taking some things out of one of our trunks. She handed me a thick, leather bound album.

'Your pressed flowers, Miss Maura.'

'Oh, Nellie,' I exclaimed. 'You kept them!' Slowly I turned over the pages. All one summer I had pressed wild flowers for Miss Schwele, my governess. They were faded and dry, and yet, looking at them now, I vividly recalled days spent searching mossy banks; days when I would wander for hours in the fields.

'Do you remember the clover field?' I asked, turning over the pages. 'Look, I pressed the most perfect specimens I could find — a white one and a pink one.'

Nellie smiled. 'You used to like to run barefoot on the grass,' she said.

'Yes, and you wouldn't allow me to,' I reminded her. 'You said young ladies didn't do that — that I was not to run about like the poor Irish children.'

'Your papa would not have liked it, Miss Maura. He expected you to behave like a lady.'

'Poor Papa . . . '

'Look, the sampler you embroidered when you were eight — the twenty-third psalm . . . '

She held it up. The silks still looked as bright as when my hot little fingers had pushed the needle through the linen.

' ''Surely goodness and mercy shall follow me all the days of my life'',' I said. 'The days of my life, Nellie! Whatever has been following me, it has not been goodness and mercy.'

I turned away, and looked through the window again. Life was going on outside. A gentleman bowed to a lady of his acquaintance in the street below; a white cat walked along with a dignified air. Two little girls skipped by, hand in hand.

'You're glad I kept everything?' asked Nellie.

'Need you ask? I can look at these things and know that there was a time when I was happy — when I ran free and wild through the grounds at Dundreary.'

'And those are the times I want you to remember. Those are the times you should remember, until you are too happy in the present to want to think of the past at all.'

'Oh, dear Lord, I've forgotten almost what happiness is — what it was,' I whispered. 'And Nellie, when were you last happy?'

'A few weeks ago. I was happy when they gave you back to me. I was happy when I nursed you back to health.' She put a few of my childhood keepsakes around the room, and packed the others carefully away again.

'Would you like me to read to you, Miss Maura?'

'I fear I have not the patience to listen,' I said. 'Embroider if you wish, Nellie. Or just talk to me while I rest. And this afternoon you must take a drive out. See about ordering a carriage; I will rest on the bed.'

'Indeed, I will not leave you! We will stay in together.'

'But you have your health to think of, Nellie.'

'I have your health to think of, too. Will you come with me, if I go for a drive?'

How cunning Nellie was. I looked at her and saw the same expression on her face as I had seen hundreds of times when she had been coaxing me to do something during my childhood.

'You know I have little alternative when you put it like that. Very well, on condition that when I do drive out, you do not expect me to wear a blue bonnet, or anything like that.'

'I promise I shan't.'

I wondered what people would think of us when we drove out together. I was struck by a sudden idea.

'Nellie, I do not wish you to be known as my maid. I mean — you can't be my nurse — surely it would be more fitting if you were my companion?'

'As you wish. Indeed, I think it is a very good idea. I am Ellen Blacklock, companion to Miss Maura Hagan, who is still in mourning for her father.'

'It's not true, really,' I said slowly. 'But yet it *is* true.'

'If you must act a lie, then it is less a lie than anything else would be.'

I sat thinking about it. A companion — yes, Nellie could carry it off quite well. Mama had been most particular that my nurse should be a refined, well-spoken woman.

'There is much of interest in Bath — much to see, and some very good concerts are held here, I believe. When you are quite recovered, we could attend some, perhaps. But there is time to think of that later.'

'Time — yes, there should be plenty of that,' I said. 'We have all the time in the world.'

Nellie made arrangements for a carriage to call at the house after luncheon. I felt a faint thrill of anticipation, mixed with fear. Travelling down in the train had been an ordeal. The unaccustomed noises, the people hurrying about on the station; the bustle and the strangeness of it all had bewildered me. But now I was stronger; calmer.

In due course I dressed for our first drive out. I knew that Nellie disliked the fact that I insisted on being veiled, but she was so pleased that I had consented to go out that she was not going to make an issue of that. When I was finally ready, we made our way downstairs, with the maid, Liza, in attendance. It was something of an occasion; the majestic Mrs Marchbanks stood in the hall, smiling. 'I am so glad you are improving, Miss Hagan,' she said.

'Thank you, Mrs Marchbanks, I am much improved.'

Nervously I stepped into the fresh brightness of a spring day, thankful for the heavy veil which hid my face. It was a relief when we were sitting in the carriage, bowling along Chippenham Crescent, past the pretty sandstone church, and out into the centre of this gracious city.

Nellie had talked a great deal about its beauty. She had already been in the abbey; I had expressed a desire to see it, and accordingly the coachman drew up close to the imposing building.

Inside, its cool dimness made a striking contrast with the brightness of the day. Great shafts of sunshine streamed in through the exquisite windows. We spoke in low voices; although lacking in formal education, Nellie enjoyed reading about places of interest. She drew my attention to the beautiful fans and pendants in the roof. There were one or two other people walking silently around. A woman in black sat praying; I felt compassion for her whatever her sorrow. When we came outside again even through my veil, the sunlight seemed blinding.

'Very impressive, isn't it?' remarked Nellie, when we were seated in the carriage again.

'Very,' I agreed.

'Are you feeling tired, Miss Maura?'

'No. I am enjoying the drive. We must visit the Roman Baths, but not today.'

'I gave the coachman instructions to drive down by the river. I thought you would enjoy that.'

We did not descend from the carriage again, but sat for a while, watching the Avon flowing sweetly along. It brought me a feeling of tranquillity. Nellie had talked of Pulteney Streety, and Milsom Street, and the bridge over the river with shops on it. Like most girls, I had delighted in going round shops once; in gazing at jewellery, material, ribbons and gloves; all the things which delight a young woman's heart. Now the mere thought of entering a shop brought feelings akin to panic.

By the time we got back to Chippenham Crescent, I felt quite tired, and yet, I was looking forward to my next trip out. Nellie was well pleased. Liza had prepared a dainty tea for us, and we sat in our sitting room and ate it.

'You are making progress,' said Nellie, as I spread some of Mrs Marchbanks' home-made jam on a scone. And I was bound to agree with her. I still tired easily, and suffered from occasional headaches, but I was improving all the time. Every afternoon, I drove out with Nellie, and as I grew stronger, we went for short walks together. At first it was quite an overwhelming experience; I had feelings of panic and insecurity, but gradually I gained more confidence.

And then I began to get an uneasy feeling that I was being watched. Whenever we went out in the carriage, I always noticed a particularly smart black one, drawn by two chestnut horses, which seemed to go wherever ours went. I mentioned this to Nellie, but she said it was just imagination on my part.

Sometimes I thought she was right, and other times I was quite positive that someone was watching my movements in Bath; watching my comings and goings from number thirty-five Chippenham Crescent. One day I noticed this carriage drive very slowly past the house.

'Look, Nellie,' I said. 'That carriage again! I won't go out today — I'm being watched, I know I am.'

'Nonsense, Miss Maura,' came the patient reply. 'Of course you are going out.'

So Nellie soothed my fears, and I continued to enjoy our outings together. I seemed to be in Bath, but not of it. It was full of distinguished people, some of whom lived there, and some who were visiting to take the waters. Eminent musicians came; many writers too, and artists whose sole occupation was painting notable members of society.

'There are so many rich, fashionable people here,' I remarked to Nellie.

'Yes . . . but you are not poor, Miss Maura,' she reminded me. That was true, but it was something which at that time I could not fully realize. One evening, greatly daring, Nellie and I attended a concert at the Pump Room. The pleasure I felt was quite indescribable; it even dimmed the memory of the recurring nightmare which had troubled me again just before waking that morning. 'You see,' said Nellie, as we came out of the Pump Room, 'you have enjoyed it immensely.'

We had arranged with our usual coachman to have the carriage waiting when we left the concert, but it was nowhere to be seen. There were quite a lot of people about, and a number of carriages waiting, but we could see no sign of ours. After a few minutes we decided it might be better if we walked home, rather than stand around in the hope our carriage would appear.

As Nellie remarked, Chippenham Crescent was not so far out of the city centre, and it was a pleasant evening.

We were about to turn and cross the road when a carriage drew up right in front of us. The coachman stepped down and raised his hat.

'Excuse me ladies. Miss Hagan and Miss Blacklock, I believe? Your coachman is unable to drive you home tonight, and I have agreed to take his place.'

'Oh,' I exclaimed, somewhat taken aback. Nellie, however, seemed to be quite composed.

'Thank you,' she said briskly. 'We were considering walking, but it will not be necessary now. Come on, Miss Maura.' But the carriage! The black carriage! I had a sudden flash of recognition; this was the carriage I had noticed before.

That dreadful dream . . . instinctively I drew back in fear, but it was too late. Nellie was already inside, and the coachman was all but bundling me in after her. The door was shut fast.

'Nellie, I don't like this — ' I began, in sudden panic, and realized there was someone else in the carriage as well.

A cry of terror rose in my throat as the coach started off, and the man sitting opposite reached forward and lifted up my veil. 'Maura!' he said. 'Maura!'

I recognized him then, and the cry died soundlessly. Blackness descended on me, and blotted out everything.

2

I was a child again, living at Dundreary House in Ireland. A child with long golden hair, and wide, wondering blue eyes. I was Maura Hagan, the only child of John Hagan, and his wife, Margaret. There was an oil painting of my mother in the entrance hall, dressed in a gold ball gown, with her fair hair piled high on her head, and great blue eyes looking out of a heart-shaped face. That was how I remembered her, elegant and beautiful, someone who always had time to listen to my childish prattle.

The nursery, so empty save for me, was in one of the attics. Looking through the window, all too often the view of lakes and mountains was obscured by rain; the brooding calm of the landscape had an atmosphere all its own. The damp green fields were shadowed by the woods, the pigeons cried mournfully into the evening dusk, and all around was the soft cadence of plaintive Irish voices.

I had parents who were truly devoted to each other, and to me. I was not banished into the nursery completely, like so many children. I saw a lot of my parents, and from an early age I was allowed to join them for dinner, dressed in white, with a blue sash round my waist, and a matching ribbon in my hair.

From birth I'd had a series of nursemaids, local young women, none of whom had pleased my mother. Finally she insisted that I should have an English nurse, a respectable woman, neither young nor flighty, nor given to drink nor any other vices.

And Nellie Blacklock came into my life, a woman of about forty, plump and kind and quiet; a woman very much alone in the world. She proceeded to give me the tender devotion and gentle discipline which my mother thoroughly approved of.

Dundreary House itself, rain-washed and weathered, was rotting away then, although I did not know that at the time. There were many servants, both in the house and out. In after years, when I had all the time in the world to think about it, I realized that my father, like most Irish landlords, was determined to keep up appearances.

He was proud of his heritage, and the name of Hagan. Our rent roll was not large; it was declining long before I was born. Looking back, I suppose we had few pleasures that cost money; as a child, my everyday clothes were woven from the wool shorn off our own sheep.

When I was seven years old, tragedy struck our household. I had been promised a baby brother or sister, and I was looking forward to it eagerly. But when I was taken to see my new brother, he was a tiny, monkey-like creature, and I was only allowed a glimpse of my mother, as she was very ill.

After that, I never saw either of them

again. For the next ten years it was just myself and Papa at Dundreary House.

My father's Uncle James and his wife, Latitia, lived a few miles away. They were a kindly couple who died within a few months of each other when I was in my eighteenth year. To my father's surprise and dismay, Uncle James died heavily in debt.

Papa went to London to attend to some of his late uncle's affairs, and it was when he returned that I noticed a change in him. He seemed withdrawn and thoughtful.

'Are you well, Papa?' I asked, when he had been back about a week.

'Yes . . . to be sure. Maura, I met a very charming lady while I was in London. A young widow, a Mrs Amelia Webber. She was staying there with friends. She lives in Northumberland with her late husband's cousin. I was talking to her about you, and she thinks you lead a very sheltered life. You are nearly eighteen now. I have been selfish; I have kept you to the home and the schoolroom. You have no real companions of your own age. It is a state of affairs that should really be remedied.'

For a moment I was too astonished to speak. Certainly my father had been doing a lot of thinking. All sorts of things appeared to have occurred to him, which I was sure he had never thought of before. It all seemed to be linked up with meeting this 'young widow'.

'I have asked Mrs Webber to visit us,' he said.

For some time now I had been doing the honours when we had visitors. As most of the people who came had known me since my childhood, I was at ease in their company. But now a little pang of fear shot through me. Papa seemed to sense it.

'You will like Mrs Webber,' he assured me. 'She has such style — such a delightful conversationalist.'

My father was looking through the window when he spoke. I turned and caught the expression on his face. It was alive, happy; something had quickened an interest in him which had not been quickened for years.

'We need new curtains in here, Maura, and one or two other things need attending to. We must arrange some entertainment for Mrs Webber — fortunately she likes riding and all country pursuits as well as the theatre.'

He peered out anxiously at the lowering hills.

'I hope it doesn't rain too much when she comes,' he went on plaintively. It was the end of a cold, wet winter, and certainly Dundreary was not looking its best. Papa gave our housekeeper instructions to refurbish the house up, and there was much scolding of maids, and polishing and cleaning.

For some time now I'd had a dress allowance, which I spent carefully under Nellie's guidance, and, up to her death, Aunt Latitia's. 'Quiet and ladylike' had been Aunt Latitia's watchwords; 'neat and tidy' were Nellie's.

Papa gave me some money, and told

me vaguely to get some nice outfits made. I went to a dressmaker in Limerick, and had a silk gown and a day dress made.

Being still in mourning for my great-uncle, I was obliged to buy dark colours. The dove-grey silk dress was far too old for me, and the low-cut style I had wanted was considered by Nellie to be 'not quite nice — your aunt would not have liked it.'

In the end, it had neither style nor cut. The day dress was no better; with the up-to-date trimmings vetoed by Nellie, it seemed to droop sadly, a porridge-coloured mess, half hidden under black crepe.

Mrs Webber arrived with her late husband's brother, Herbert Webber, and her French maid, Cosette. Amelia Webber was tall, with a very shapely figure, and luxuriant fair hair, which she wore elaborately dressed. Herbert Webber was about thirty, I thought. He was short, and powerfully built. He walked with a slight limp, and had some sort of back deformity which gave him a very hunched appearance. I soon learnt that this in no way detracted from his prowess as a sportsman.

He bowed over my hand, and held it a good deal longer than was necessary. He had thin, reddish hair, small eyes, and a face and head which seemed too large for his body. I felt an immediate aversion to him.

At dinner that evening, Mrs Webber sat opposite my father, her beautifully cut, wine-coloured gown enhancing the lines of her figure. With a sense of shock, I saw the admiration in Papa's eyes.

'Did you arrange the flowers yourself, Miss Hagan?' enquired her brother-in-law.

'I did indeed, sir,' I replied, blushing.

'Then you have done it beautifully. Your daughter is a credit to you,' he said, turning to my father.

'I'm afraid I can't claim much credit,' said Papa, taking his eyes away from Amelia for a moment. 'Her nurse, Nellie, has been worth her weight in gold. And she has had a very good governess — a German girl, Miss Schwele. My aunt, who unfortunately died recently, always kept an eye on her, too.'

'A German governess, however worthy, cannot instruct in the social graces, or give the companionship and example to be found in a really good establishment for young ladies. Education is not just a matter of remembering dates — not that I ever could — or knowing the exact position of places on a map.'

Having expressed her opinion on education, Mrs Webber sipped her wine thoughtfully. School had never been mentioned in our house; I knew that Papa was well pleased with my progress under Miss Schwele. To my surprise, he nodded approvingly when Amelia had finished speaking.

'I suppose we are in rather a rut here,' he said. 'A pleasant one, of course. But it's selfish of me to keep Maura in one.'

'I venture to suggest that Miss Hagan will not be in a rut for very long — indeed, as she is not yet eighteen, she can scarcely be said to be in one at all, yet.'

Mr Webber was drinking wine freely. He smiled at me as he spoke, but there was something peculiarly unpleasant about that smile; something curiously insinuating in his words.

'You must both come and stay at Battle Tower in Northumberland,' said Amelia. 'Uncle Basil will be delighted to meet you.'

When the meal was over, Amelia and I retired to the drawing room.

'Would you like me to play the piano for you?' I asked nervously.

'Not particularly, dear child. I would rather talk to you.' She walked restlessly around the room, her critical gaze taking everything in. 'You have the faintest trace of Irish brogue,' she said. 'You and your father. It is not unattractive. You resemble your mother — I noticed that as soon as I saw her portrait. You are not very tall, so it is important that you stand erect. You have good features — ' she broke off. 'I hope you don't mind my saying all this.'

'Not at all,' I said slowly, getting over my first feeling of surprise that she would make such personal remarks. I had never met a woman like this before, who, although intelligent besides being attractive, thought that to look beautiful was almost a necessity. To be well dressed; to have 'style', to know the exact way to wear everything; clearly she regarded what Aunt Latitia used to call 'frivolities' as anything but.

'No one has ever talked to me about these sort of things,' I added.

'Exactly what I suspected. You are a girl who could be a great beauty, if you were shown how to make the best of yourself. Many doors will open to you, if you want them to.'

Under the compelling charm of her personality, I forgot my unbecoming dress; my shyness went. She asked me questions about my father, and about myself and the life we led at Dundreary House. And she told me about her life at Battle Tower.

She had lived there for the past two years. She told me she had been widowed for five years, her young husband having died of pneumonia. The man she called Uncle Basil was her late husband's cousin, once removed. Apparently Basil Webber had made a great deal of money abroad, where he had married a rich but ailing wife.

He had finally returned to England, where he bought a lot of property in Northumberland, including Battle Tower. His wife being in such poor health, he had his widowed cousin, Martha, to help run the establishment, along with her unmarried son, Herbert.

'Oddly enough, she is a cousin of his who married a cousin, so you could say she's a Webber twice over,' said Amelia, with a rather enigmatic smile.

As Amelia was also a widow, he asked her if she would care to make Battle Tower her home, too. Having no children of his own, and his closest blood relations being Martha and her son, Amelia said having them there gave him the feeling of being a family man. She said that when he asked her to live there, she hesitated at first, because she had never really cared for her mother-in-law, Martha Webber. She said she got on very well with Basil Webber, though.

While we were talking thus, the door opened, and my father and Herbert Webber appeared. Papa glanced at me fondly, and then his gaze rested on Amelia. Her eyes seemed to beckon him. Young as I was, I saw very clearly that he was infatuated with this woman. As to Amelia's feelings for him . . . I could never truly say. But whatever they were, she meant to have him.

I cannot deny that I enjoyed the Webbers' stay immensely. The four of us went to every possible place of interest and entertainment that Papa could think of.

True, I did not care for Herbert Webber, although his behaviour towards me was always correct. Amelia and my father were together when we went any-where, so Herbert was bound to attend on me, as any gentleman would. When they finally left us to return to England, it was on the understanding that we would visit Battle Tower as soon as possible.

'Ireland is charming — and so peaceful,' Amelia remarked to me, on their last evening at Dundreary House. 'But it's about a hundred years behind England in practically everything.'

There was something curiously ominous about that remark.

About two days after our guests had gone, I sat thinking about it when a maid entered the room with a hasty message from Clancy, the coachman, for me to go to the stables. Instinctively I knew it was to do with my beloved old pony, Rory. I dashed out of the house, through the servants' quarters and into the stable-yard, to be met by a grim-faced Clancy.

'I'm afraid it's too late, Miss Maura. It's Rory — he just laid down — poor ould creature — and gave a few gasps — and — it was all over . . .'

3

My first impression of Battle Tower was of a place grim and ancient, stone-built and forbidding, with the bastions of the Cheviots rising in the distance. After a long and exhausting journey, Amelia and Mr Basil Webber had met our train at Alnwick, and taken us the rest of the way by carriage.

As we drove through the lodge gates, Papa read out the Latin inscription on them: '*Quod Habemus Id Tenemus*. What we have we hold . . . I believe that is the correct translation, Mr Webber?'

'Quite so,' agreed our host. There was just a trace of embarrassment in his voice.

That was the family motto, then. As we entered the house, I noticed it again above the great oaken door, and under it, two other words: *Justus Heres*. Papa, although something of a Latin scholar, did not comment again. When we entered the stone-flagged hall, we were met by the glassy-eyed stare of an enormous white bull, stuffed and standing on a high wooden platform. I had never seen anything like it in my life. Papa too was clearly interested, but Amelia burst out laughing at our amazed faces.

'It's from the wild white Chillingham herd of cattle,' explained our host at dinner that evening.

'Was it shot?' I asked timidly.

'Indeed, no, Miss Hagan. Nobody is allowed to hunt or molest the cattle in any way. The herd is very ancient — the only white one in the world, I believe. That bull strayed away from the herd and died — perhaps it had been driven away by the leader bull — we don't know. But the family who lived here before us — um — the Ancrofts — '

He paused a moment. 'The Ancrofts got possession of it somehow, and — er — I liked it, and they were willing to part with certain things . . .'

His voice trailed away, as though what he was saying was somehow embarrassing to him. He was a tall man, with sandy hair and a moustache fading to a sort of pepper-and-salt. I judged him to be somewhat older than my father. He had small grey eyes with which he scanned me in a very personal way; indeed, he seemed to be very interested in all my affairs.

His wife was not at the dinner-table; she was in very poor health, and confined to her room. He explained briefly that she was not well enough to meet people. His widowed cousin, Martha, was there, though. She was a tall, gaunt woman of about sixty years, with the little eyes which all the Webbers seemed to possess. She had a tight-lipped mouth which rarely smiled; I knew instinctively that she did not approve of Amelia, still less of the romance which was obviously going on between her daughter-in-law and my father. Amelia sat, looking splendid as usual, smiling at Papa, while Herbert

Webber darted smirking glances across at me.

Sitting at that elegant table, in that splendid room, eating the rich food, and sipping wine, one thing was very clear to me. I did not care for Mr Basil Webber at all, nor for his cousin Martha — and least of all for her son, Herbert. I felt vaguely guilty about this, but I could not help it.

Nellie had travelled with us as my maid, and Papa had brought his valet with him.

My room was beautiful, facing onto the drive and parkland at the front of the house. A large coal fire burnt in the hearth, the hangings on the four-poster bed were of crimson brocade, and the furniture was dark oak. There was a writing table equipped with every-thing one could possibly use, even to sheets of various stamps. The marble-topped washstand had a double set of ewers and basins on it.

Stags horns bristled from the walls of the long corridors, and the skins of animals lay on the stone floors. Grimly forbidding outside, luxurious and beautiful inside, Battle Tower was the home of a very rich man.

'There's a keen wind,' commented Nellie, looking through the window of my room the following morning. 'But the air is fresh and bracing, and the sky is blue.'

'Do you like it, Nellie?' I asked, standing beside her at the window. 'Battle Tower, I mean.'

'Well, Miss Maura, it's very grand — very grand indeed. In the servants' hall here, they say Mr Webber's wife is very ill — and he has no children. They say his cousin is his heir — but they say — '

I burst out laughing. 'They say a lot in the servants' hall by the sound of it,' I said. 'What else do they say?'

'They say there will be an announcement of a forth-coming wedding before this visit is over.' She slipped her arm around me.

'I think they are probably right,' I

said. 'Papa has as good as told me so — well, at least, told me they are fond of each other. I think he has made up his mind to marry Mrs Amelia as the servants call her. And with no-fewer than three Mrs Webbers in the house, they must be hard put to know what to call each one.'

'They say Mr Webber's wife is always heavily veiled,' said Nellie. 'Even in the house — even in her room.'

'In the house — in her room,' I repeated. 'Whatever for?'

'She lived in India, where Mr Webber married her. They say her family was very wealthy, but that she was mauled by a tiger when she was a child! Somehow she recovered and lived. But they say her face is terrible — and part of one arm — ' Nellie gave a shudder — 'missing altogether. Of late years she has been in ill-health — and not herself, either.' She tapped her head significantly.

'Oh, how dreadful! Poor lady,' I said. And at that moment despite the fact that I felt unable to like him, a certain feeling of pity for Mr Webber stirred inside me.

The following day we went driving; Amelia, Mr Webber, Papa and myself. The Border country was beautiful; wild and lonely and rugged. The charming little village of Witton lay about two miles from Battle Tower.

Battle Tower was named thus, I learnt, because of the many battles between the Scots and the English which had taken place in the vicinity. On the way back, something startled the horses as we turned a narrow lane. The carriage, a four-wheeled brougham, jerked suddenly, and shot forward, swaying alarmingly from side to side.

'Keep calm,' said Mr Webber. 'The coachman will soon get control again.' It was obvious, though, that the horses had bolted. The carriage hurtled along at a terrific speed; I was too petrified to scream, and I think Amelia was, too. It was all confusion, the twisting, creaking carriage, the frantic clatter of hooves, and the coachman and groom shouting.

I caught a swift glimpse of a man on horseback; there was more shouting from the coachman and groom, and the next I saw through the window was a riderless horse. I gave an involuntary cry, and felt suddenly sick.

And then, almost imperceptibly at first, the pace of the vehicle slowed down, and finally drew to a shuddering halt. For a moment we sat there, shaken and speechless. Then the coachman climbed down and opened the carriage door.

'I'm sorry about that, sir, but we couldn't have stopped them! There might have been a nasty accident if it hadn't been for young Mr Ancroft — '

Embarrassment showed plainly on Mr Webber's face.

'Oh! Young Ancroft stopped them, did he?' he muttered, half to himself. He stepped down from the carriage and with one accord we all followed him.

The horses stood panting, wet with sweat, lips foam-flecked, eyes still rolling wildly. A young man was astride one, gentling it, while the groom soothed and calmed the other animal.

'Aye,' said the coachman, in the strange Northumbrian accent which I was hard put to understand. 'Mr Ancroft saw what was happening. Fortunately he was on horseback ahead of us, sir, so he prepared to ride alongside, and throw hisself on Marrer's back. I've never seen owt like it, and that's a fact. It was that dog barking that frightened 'em — just sprang out of the hedge, like. Mind, that's the best bit of horsemanship I've seen in many a long day.'

The young man dismounted. He was dark-haired, slim, and fairly tall. He had a sensitive face, with a high forehead and hazel eyes. A deep cleft softened the firmness of his chin. He was hatless, having no doubt lost it during his wild ride.

He too looked, if not embarrassed, a trifle taken aback on seeing Mr Webber.

'Mr Ancroft, I wish to offer my

44

thanks on behalf of myself and my companions. Stopping the horses like that was a very fine and courageous thing to do. We have two ladies in the carriage as you can see.'

The young man bowed in our direction. 'It was a natural thing to do under the circumstances,' he said quietly. 'I hope it was not too distressing an experience for them.' He glanced at Amelia and me, his gaze catching mine, and holding it.

'You are already acquainted with Mrs Amelia Webber — may I introduce Lieutenant Charles Ancroft, a neighbour of ours. This is Mr John Hagan and his daughter, Miss Maura — they are on a visit from Ireland.'

The young man smiled, bowed, and murmured the correct greetings, but I wondered why a look of pain had crossed his face when Mr Webber had called him 'a neighbour of ours'. Admiration, interest, curiosity, all stirred in me at the same time.

'We are expecting to give a ball

before our guests return to Ireland,' went on Mr Webber. 'I take it you are on leave. Perhaps you and your brother could attend? If your brother is — um — not well enough, you yourself will be very welcome. We will be issuing invitations shortly.'

'Thank you. I will consult my brother. I am stationed close at hand at the moment,' replied the young man. Again his eyes met mine. I had the feeling that Mr Webber, though thankful someone had stopped the runaway horses, would have preferred it not to have been Charles Ancroft. Just at that moment, a grey, riderless horse appeared round the bend in the lane, and trotted towards us.

'My faithful mount,' exclaimed our rescuer, smiling. It was a gay, sunny smile, and lighted up his whole face. We waited to see him mount his horse again, and then, murmuring our thanks once more, we got back into the carriage.

'Well,' remarked Amelia, as we set off

at a careful pace, 'we were fortunate indeed that Mr Ancroft did the right thing — or should I call him Lieutenant Ancroft? So odd sounding somehow, unless a man is wearing uniform.'

'It was certainly a surprise when I saw who our rescuer was,' said Mr Webber.

'He was no doubt rather surprised himself when he saw who he had rescued.' There was something faintly malicious in Amelia's voice as she said that.

'He seems a fine young man. They are neighbours of yours then, the Ancrofts?' enquired Papa.

'They live a couple of miles away, at The Little Manor House,' explained Mr Webber. 'As a matter of fact, I bought Battle Tower from them — and a good deal of what is in it, too. Michael Ancroft, the elder brother — well — his debts were enormous. No need to go into all the sordid details, of course. I wanted Battle Tower, and I was prepared to pay for it. Young Charles has no choice but the army, I suppose. A bad business for him, no doubt.'

He dismissed the Ancroft family from the conversation then. Later, as we entered the house, I glanced up at the family motto, and the two words written beneath: '*Justus Heres*'.

Papa had told me that it meant the 'rightful heir'. Well whoever was the rightful heir to Battle Tower, somehow I could not feel that it was this cold-eyed man who had bought it, and who had asked his cousins to live there. Undoubtedly he was a man who wanted his power to be felt by those around him.

Nevertheless, he was very kind and attentive to both Papa and me. Preparations went ahead for the ball. Papa had told me that he and Amelia were announcing their engagement at it.

My feelings were mixed. Naturally, I did not like to think that anyone was taking my place in Papa's affections, but he told me that was impossible. He pointed out that Amelia was young and full of life, that she would make an ideal chaperon for me, and draw me out of the too-quiet life I was leading.

He also said that he thought school for a year or two in England would be a very good idea, and then, possibly, I might attend some good establishment for young ladies in France.

'Amelia opened my eyes to my duties towards a young daughter. It would be wrong of me to tie you to the home too closely. At least you should have the opportunity of attending a good school, both in England and in France.'

'School in England,' I began dubiously. 'Where?'

'I believe there is an excellent school near Scarborough. Amelia knows all about it.'

'It's a long way from Ireland,' I said.

Papa looked slightly uncomfortable. 'Ireland is not the only place in the world to live in.'

'What do you mean, Papa? Surely it is the only place for us?'

'Dundreary is just a millstone round

my neck now, Maura. Oh, I love it in the same way that you do, but there is no future for us there. Uncle James left nothing but a mass of debts . . . '

He paused, and then went on. 'There is a charming house a few miles away from here. It's called Wild Witton. Through Mr Webber's influence I can have that place. My dear, it is better for you, for me — and for Amelia, if we leave Ireland before things get any worse. Believe me, I have given plenty of thought to the matter.'

Although he spoke gently, I felt a sense of shock, of being torn up by the roots.

'And what of Nellie?' I asked.

'I've no doubt some of our servants will want to come to England with us, and some will not. But whatever happens, Nellie stays with us as your maid. And when you go to school, well, we can arrange for her to have some light duties until such time as your education is complete.' I realized then that the matter had been well thought out and talked over, before it had been mentioned to me. I felt mingled grief and resentment. My whole life was changing, and I had little doubt as to who had instigated these changes.

Outwardly, though, these were Papa's wishes, and there was nothing I could do except fall in with them. I broke the news to Nellie that we were leaving Ireland, and going to live at Wild Witton. The wedding was to take place in the summer, and I would start school in the Autumn term.

'Oh, Miss Maura,' said Nellie, clinging to me. 'Never mind, my lamb, I'll still be with you. And when you go to school, I'll write as often as you want.'

'I'm glad Rory's dead,' I said bitterly.

4

I was in Amelia's room at Battle Tower. Everywhere was littered with clothes, and from the adjoining dressing-room came the smell of scorched paper, where her maid, Cosette, was preparing the curling tongs. It was the day of the ball, and as I really had no suitable gown, according to fashion-conscious Amelia, she was going through her own wardrobe to see if she had anything I could wear.

'This is last season's, Maura — but it is a lovely dress. Try it on.'

Obediently I took off my plain cotton wrapper, and Amelia slipped the garment over my head. It was a soft shade of blue, which suited me perfectly.

'It's too tight round the waist,' I said.

'Nonsense! You're not laced properly. I suppose nobody has seen to these things — you need a French maid. I was twelve when I started to wear stays. Cosette, lace Miss Hagan properly.'

I stood meekly while Cosette drew the laces tighter.

'You'll get used to it,' said Amelia consolingly, as I gave a stifled gasp. 'Now fasten her up, Cosette.'

A moment later I stood in front of the mirror, with the critical gaze of the other two on me.

'It's a bit long,' said Amelia. 'Apart from that, it's a perfect fit. Do you like it?'

'It's beautiful,' I said. And indeed, to a girl unused to any style at all, the effect was breathtaking.

'Take up the hem, Cosette.'

'*Oui, madame.*'

In spite of the shock of being told we were leaving Ireland, and knowing that my life would change completely when my father re-married, yet I was looking forward to the ball that evening. Fortunately I'd had dancing lessons, although I had never attended a ball before, and shyly told Amelia so.

'Your gown should *really* be white,' she said. 'But it's of no consequence. Would you like Cosette to do your hair? That maid of yours, Nellie, was a good and kind nurse, no doubt, but a proper lady's maid must know how to dress hair in the latest style. If Nellie watches Cosette, she will soon learn, and it is right that she should, Maura.'

Amelia had told me that she understood what an awful wrench it would be for me to leave Dundreary, but that under the circumstances it was better for all of us.

'It is the beginning of a wonderful new life for you, Maura. You see if I'm not right.'

I was surprised at the number of people who attended the ball, some of them staying on as house guests. Mr Webber's wife was not present, of course; his cousin, Martha Webber, was the official hostess, although it was Amelia, radiant in an amethyst-coloured gown, who dominated the scene.

My heart gave an unexpected little

thump when the guests foregathered in the drawing room, and among them I recognized our rescuer, Charles Ancroft. With Nellie watching carefully, Cosette had dressed my hair high on my head, giving my appearance a new maturity.

I wore a gold locket and chain which had been my mother's, but despite this, and the lovely gown I was wearing, I still felt somewhat shy among so many strangers. One of the people I was introduced to was Michael Ancroft, Charles' elder brother.

He looked about twenty years his senior, and entirely unlike him, a sallow, gaunt man, whose eyes roved restlessly around the room.

There was the buzz of voices everywhere; animated greetings from people who had not met for some time. I heard snatches of conversations about hunting and shooting, about weddings and brides, and every so often lowered voices; a whisper behind a fan as something confidential was discussed.

Some of the dowager ladies did not

always lower their voices enough.

' . . . yes, they are going to live at Wild Witton . . . no doubt Mr Webber regards him as a good connection . . . fine looking man. As regards her . . . ' The voice dropped then, but I distinctly heard the word 'adventuress'. Then another lady began talking.

'Both the Ancroft brothers here; I don't know how they must feel. Well, I don't think Michael cares about anything now. One can't snub Webber, I suppose . . . you can buy a lot, but you can't buy breeding. He may live here, but he doesn't belong here, my dear, and everybody knows it, even though they may accept his hospitality. I think Charles Ancroft has come mainly to keep an eye on his brother. Just as well Charles is in the army. What else is there for him now, poor boy?'

The speaker paused for breath, and then continued.

'Michael might not have gone to pieces if that flighty wife of his hadn't run off with someone else . . . yes, my dear! They say he's drinking himself to death . . . yes, and when he dies, by rights, Battle Tower would belong to Charles. But can you imagine . . . an Ancroft *selling* it like that? When Michael does die, what an inheritance for anyone!'

There was a moment's silence. It was impossible for me to move without making myself conspicuous, and the next minute the speaker began again.

'Talking of inheritance, Mr Webber seems singularly unfortunate in that respect. That wife of his — well, my dear, if a man marries for money . . . yes . . . without an heir, in spite of everything. That cousin sticks as close as a clam, of course . . . ' Feeling a mixure of distaste and curiosity, I managed to edge myself away.

The supper was set out and served in the banqueting room. Although it was a very large room, not all the guests could be seated. Cold chicken, lobster patties, game pie; meringues, trifles; every imaginable sweet and savoury was served, and there was champagne to drink. The butler, footmen, and parlourmaid were all busy serving, and the buzz of conversation grew louder and louder. It was quelled eventually by Mr Webber announcing the forthcoming marriage between my father and Amelia.

A little pang of sadness struck through me when he spoke. To my surprise, I caught Charles Ancroft's eye, and he gave me an understanding and encouraging smile.

I felt better straight away. Papa made a short speech, in which he said he would soon be leaving Ireland to make his home in Northumberland, where, he said, he expected to be very happy. Toasts were drunk, there were many congratulations, and my father and Amelia were showered with good wishes.

As the guests mixed and mingled, I saw Charles Ancroft moving towards me; in the distance I could hear the musicians tuning up in the long gallery.

'Are you feeling a trifle neglected, Miss Hagan?' came a voice at my elbow. Unnoticed, my host, Mr Webber, had slipped into the seat beside me, a few seconds after it had been vacated.

'Not at all, thank you, sir,' I replied primly, feeling a little vexed that he had beaten Charles to it.

'I am sure you are eager for the dancing to start, like most young ladies. But I hear this is your first ball.'

'It is,' I admitted, blushing a little.

'Then I am honoured that it is taking place in my house. And for the same reason, I would like to book two dances now, before your engagement card is full. You are so young and fresh and unspoilt; the more one sees of life, and the older one grows, the more rare and precious these qualities seem.'

I handed him my card without speaking.

'You have not yet seen Wild Witton, I believe?'

'Not yet, sir.'

'You will like it very much. Ireland is a beautiful country, no doubt, but hardly the place for a young lady like you.'

'Why not?' I was curious.

'Because you are on the point of turning into a great beauty, and you demand another setting. Ireland is too remote — ' He paused.

'But when one is living in Ireland, England seems remote,' I said.

'You do not care for the idea of living here, then?'

Loyalty to my father guarded my reply. 'I cannot really say. People grow attached to the homes they were born and brought up in.'

'That is is true, no doubt. But at your age, a change should be a challenge.'

'Well, I suppose so . . . ' The champagne was going to my head, just a little.

'Doubtless you are looking forward to your own wedding day, Miss Hagan.'

'I hadn't thought about it.'

'I expect your father has, though. He will want you to make a good match.'

Somehow this conversation was becoming distasteful. Mr Webber's face was flushed, and it was all to close to mine.

'My wife is in very poor health.' He spoke almost abruptly.

'Yes, I had heard so. I am very sorry.'

'I have no children; no son of my own to inherit.'

Why was he telling me all this? I sat with my eyes downcast, aware of his keen gaze.

'You will be starting school later this year, I believe?'

Somehow I resented the too personal interest he seemed to be taking in my affairs. As I was accepting his hospitality, though, I could do nothing but reply.

'It is not yet arranged, but I am expecting to.'

'That will be another big change for you.'

For a few minutes longer he talked to me in a similar vein, and then he was obliged to give his attention to other guests.

Charles approached and bowed, smiling down at me. 'Good evening, Miss Hagan. I trust you felt no ill effects after your somewhat alarming drive the other day?'

I laughed. 'None at all. It is funny to look back on now, although it was frightening at the time. We were lucky that you were out riding, and that you behaved with such courage and presence of mind.'

A good many of the guests had already drifted into the gallery, attracted by the sound of music. Charles sat down in the seat Mr Webber had vacated.

'It was nothing, although I'm very glad I was able to stop the horses. I understand you are leaving Ireland, Miss Hagan, and coming to live at Wild Witton.'

'Yes,' I said.

'And you are perhaps a little sad?'

'How did you know?'

'Who would not be? When one has lived and grown up in one house — ' He broke off, and glanced round the room.

I thought of the snatches of conversation I had overheard about him and his brother.

'I'd never imagined living anywhere but Dundreary House, up to Papa meeting Mrs Webber,' I said.

'So all this has been very sudden?'

'Very sudden indeed.'

'If you must leave a house you love, and live elsewhere, it is often better to move away altogether, than to still see it, and know that it is no longer your home.'

As he spoke I sensed that there was deep emotion behind his words, and I knew that he was thinking of his own position regarding Battle Tower.

'Being in the army, I am seldom in Northumberland as a rule. At the moment I am stationed not far away, so I have been home more frequently.'

'I shall miss Ireland dreadfully, I know,' I said. 'I'm sure Papa will, too, but he says it is for the best. Indeed, he says it's the only course open to him since his uncle died, and left nothing but debts.'

'Ah, yes; circumstances compel people to do these things, Miss Hagan.'

'And there is nothing I can do — nothing at all,' I said, not without some bitterness.

'Nothing. Three years ago I watched my brother dispose of Battle Tower to the highest bidder, and there was nothing *I* could do. We come here as guests — guests!'

The outraged frustration in his voice made me realize how intensely he resented his position. Something in the obstinate set of his mouth and chin made me feel that, had Battle Tower been his, whatever the problems, whatever the hardships to be endured, or the sacrifices to be made, he would never have parted with it.

The more bitter it must be for him to know that Battle Tower had been sold because of his brother's excesses, if the gossip I had overheard was true. And I had an idea it was; already Michael Ancroft's face was flushed with drink; he looked a sick, unhappy man, his eyes endlessly roving around the great room we were gathered in, and which should by rights be his.

'I'm so sorry. I mean, sorry that your home was sold, and that you could do nothing about it,' I said. 'It is a lovely place, although at first I thought it was rather grim looking. Papa says the family motto means 'What we have we hold'. And the other words over the door, *Justus Heres* — and I see, over the fireplace in here — they mean — '

'The rightful heir,' said Charles. 'The rightful heir being an Ancroft. My ancestors were fierce fighters, by all accounts. If you haven't been in the tapestry room yet, make a point of going. Michael left some tapestries here at Webber's request. They depict various Border scuffles — and you will notice *Justus Heres* worked on all of them. There is an ancient legend, curse — call it what you will — that says that no man, be he English or Scot, will ever take Battle Tower away from the rightful heir. The curse will fall upon any man who tries, and he will never have an heir of his own.'

There was something menacing about his voice as he told me this; I wondered if he himself believed the old legend. I thought of Mr Webber's words: 'I have no children; no son of my own to inherit'.

'I am sorry, Miss Hagan. The conversation is becoming very serious, and this is an engagement ball! If I may book two dances — '

'With pleasure,' I said, smiling, handing him my card.

'I would like to book more, but — ' He gave a resigned little smile. To dance with a young man more than twice at any function would give rise to gossip. Even so, my engagement card was soon full; I was by no means a wallflower, a fact which Amelia afterwards remarked upon, knowing that I had been rather shy at the beginning of the evening.

Dancing with Charles was a heady experience. Somehow we had already established a certain link between us even on such short acquaintance. We had exchanged confidences about how we felt concerning our respective positions. Waltzing with him, I had the sensation almost of floating around the room. We said little during that first dance, but I felt a happiness in his arms which made me forget for the time being the big changes I would be facing before long.

Very different were my feelings as I danced with Herbert Webber.

'How delightful you look tonight, Miss Hagan. No wonder you are so popular as a dancing partner. As you are coming to live in the Border country, the sooner you meet these people, the better. Undoubtedly your presence will brighten up Wild Witton.'

Although what he said was not in itself offensive, it was the peculiarly familar way in which he said it. I could not explain why, but I felt a shrinking distaste at having to be in such close proximity.

'Women are indeed perverse creatures,' he went on. 'My mother never cared for Amelia when my brother married her, nor was she pleased when

Amelia came to live at Battle Tower. But now that she is to re-marry, and leave here to be mistress of Wild Witton, she is still displeased! I cannot think what Mother would have her do, but the fair Amelia cares nothing for her opinion, anyway. In my experience, what Amelia wants, Amelia gets.' He gave an unpleasant laugh, and squeezed my hand as the dance ended. I did not enjoy it, nor did I enjoy dancing with my host.

'You will miss Amelia when she gets married,' I said, feeling bound to make conversation, and not wishing it to turn on me again. Both Papa and Amelia had said they wanted me to call her by her Christian name.

'I will in many ways,' he agreed. 'But on the other hand, Wild Witton is not far away.'

'I have not yet seen it.'

'But you will before you return to Ireland. Having your father living there, and Amelia, will make it a place for family gatherings. Your father will soon be well known and popular here, coming from such an old Irish family — '

He broke off, and I was unpleasantly reminded of the conversation I had overheard in the drawing room. I had a feeling that somehow the people in this house were scheming for their own ends. What was going on in Battle Tower, behind the façade of the Webber's hospitality?

5

Wild Witton was quite an attractive looking dwelling, I was bound to admit. It was brick-built, which I had somehow not expected, but ivy almost obscured the brickwork on the front of the house. It lacked the mellow, if somewhat crumbling beauty of Dundreary House, and of course, it lacked the impressive splendour of Battle Tower.

'A gentleman's residence,' was Papa's comment.

It was not large, but it had spacious, pleasant rooms, and it was set in a small but attractive parkland. It had been empty for several months, the previous owners having gone abroad.

Amelia seemed delighted as the lodge-keeper handyman showed us around. She was like a child with a new toy, exclaiming how attractive the view was from the window, what a splendid staircase, and what a lot of entertaining she intended to do. Mr Webber walked around with an appraising air, occasionally casting an indulgent glance at Amelia. While we were inspecting the servants' hall, he unexpectedly turned and asked me what I thought of it.

'It's quite a nice house,' I said, a trifle lamely.

'When all your personal belongings are here; when it is furnished in style, I think you will like it very much, Miss Hagan. Your father has some fine horses, I understand. When your stables are full, it will seem like home to you — you see.'

'You are kind to say so,' I replied. 'My pony, Rory, died this year. He was very old — I can't remember life without him.'

'I have a splendid chestnut mare, Josty, which I would be delighted to give you,' he said quickly. 'You must see her, Miss Hagan.'

I could feel myself flushing with embarrassment.

'Thank you. You are very kind, Mr Webber, but I really cannot accept such a gift — '

'You can, Miss Hagan! I shall have a word with your father — indeed, I should be gravely offended if you refused my gift. I hope to be your friend, my dear, and your father's friend.'

He put his hand under my elbow as we ascended the stairs from the servants' quarters. I disliked the physical contact, slight though it was, nor did I like the idea of taking the gift of a horse from him. Yet I knew I would be obliged to do so if Papa did not object. I confided these thoughts in the understanding Nellie.

I had told her all about Wild Witton; before returning to Ireland we were going to take her and Papa's valet, O'Neal, to see it.

'We passed another house on the way to Wild Witton,' I told her. 'They call it The Little Manor House. It's quite small and shabby looking, Nellie. I couldn't believe it when Amelia pointed it out, and said the Ancroft brothers now lived there. Imagine that! And their family owned Battle Tower for generations.'

'Funny things seem to go on in these parts,' said Nellie darkly. 'I don't know how I shall settle down here when you go to school, and that's a fact.'

One afternoon, a day or two before we left Battle Tower, I was going along the corridor to my room, when a sudden impulse made me turn in a different direction and walk along a passage where I had not been before. I had seen a good deal of the place, but it was so vast and rambling that a large number of rooms were never used at all.

It was at the front of the house; just a series of closed doors, and then some stairs leading onto the next floor. I hesitated between going up them, or retracing my footsteps. Finally, I decided to go up them. It was just curiosity, for what could be there except more empty rooms?

Sure enough, there was a smaller

passage, with closed doors. Nothing of interest. I turned, and was on the point of coming downstairs again, when I heard a woman's voice coming from one of the rooms.

'Alice! Is that you, Alice? I've been ringing . . . Alice! Alice!'

I stood with my heart thumping, not sure what to do. Then I heard the voice again. I turned back and tapped on the door where it seemed to be coming from. There was no reply, but I heard movements from within. The door was slowly opened, and a woman stood there. She was wearing a very beautiful crimson wrapper, trimmed with white swansdown. A thick black veil shrouded her head and shoulders completely.

I realized straight away that this was the unfortunate Mrs Webber, and these were her apartments in the house.

'I beg your pardon,' I said. 'I just happened to walk up the stairs, and heard you call. Can I be of any assistance to you? I am a guest here — you must be Mrs Webber? I am so sorry you are too ill to receive people. My name is Maura Hagan.' For a moment she did not reply, and I stood there, feeling very ill at ease.

'Yes, I am Mrs Webber,' she said at last. 'Come into my room. Let me look at you.'

She opened the door wide, and I entered, somewhat reluctantly. The room was spacious and beautiful. Bookshelves lined all one wall, and in front of the fire a grey Persian cat sprawled indolently. It was evidently a sitting room, containing a piano, comfortable chairs, and much bric-à-brac; carved ivory elephants and figurines were grouped around. I noticed another door in the room, and guessed that must be her bedroom.

'I know there are guests in the house,' she said. 'There has been a ball, hasn't there?'

'Yes.'

'And you danced?'

'Yes. It was very nice indeed. I wish you could have attended it.'

'Be seated,' she said, indicating a

chair. 'Tell me all about it. Who was there?'

I was obliged to recount to her the details of the ball, in which she was very interested.

'I am coming to live at Wild Witton shortly,' I said. 'Are you sure there is nothing I can do for you, Mrs Webber? You were calling for Alice.'

'My maid. She'll be here directly. She spends a good deal of time with me. She'll be having tea in the servants' hall now. She knows I get lonely, and ring the bell a few minutes after she leaves me.'

'I would have come and talked to you before, Mrs Webber, had I known you were well enough,' I said. I suddenly noticed that one sleeve of her wrapper hung loose and empty. Her manner seemed to change quite suddenly. She gave a loud, rather jarring laugh.

'Would you?' she said. 'Would you? Well, you had better go now anyway.'

She stood up. 'How nice to know that you have enjoyed my company,' she said, following me to the door. She laughed again. 'Look!'

To my horror, she slowly lifted up her veil, and revealed a face so hideous, so mutilated, that it scarcely seemed human. The terrible, twisted mouth grimaced in a smile; the one eye stared at me above a network of scars. I gasped; she gave another strident laugh, and dropped her veil again. The next moment I was over the threshold, the door was shut, and I was hurrying down the stairs and away from that part of the house as fast as I could.

6

I shall never forget the excitement of that spring and summer, although my feelings, were very mixed. I wept when we finally left Dundreary, and made the crossing to our new home in England.

I wept the first night I slept in Wild Witton, and wept again when I looked through the window in the morning, and saw the unfamiliar landscape. I believe Papa was upset too, but like me, he was swept forward with plans for the wedding.

Amelia was to be married in a cream-coloured costume, and have four attendants. I was one of them, the other three being young cousins of hers who lived in the county of Durham.

In a silk gown of palest blue, with a heart-shaped neckline and tiny waist, I stood and saw my father marry Amelia Webber in the lovely old church at

Witton. It was crowded with guests, and beautifully decorated with flowers from the green-houses at Battle Tower. Basil Webber gave her away, and a friend of my father's came from Ireland to be best man. Herbert Webber was there, casting surreptitious glances at me. His mother, tight-lipped, cold-eyed, dressed in a particularly unbecoming shade of steel grey, was there, I suspected, for the sake of appearances.

Afterwards we were given a sumptuous wedding breakfast at Battle Tower. Both the Ancroft brothers were there, and Charles' eyes soon sought mine again. Before long he was at my side.

'Miss Hagan! You are now living at Wild Witton — we are neighbours.'

'We are indeed,' I said. 'Soon I shall be starting school, though, so I'll not be spending much time here.'

'Where will you be going to school?'

'In Yorkshire. A place near Scarborough. I don't know it at all.'

'I do. It is very pleasant there.'

'I start in September, so I have a few

weeks at Wild Witton first.'

'I'm still in camp at Otterburn, so I get home quite often. I hope we may meet.'

'My new stepmother intends to entertain a lot, I believe,' I said. 'She is convinced that I have led too quiet a life in Ireland. I'm sure we will meet.'

'They will be going on honeymoon now, I suppose?'

'Yes. To Paris.'

'And what will you do? Stay alone at Wild Witton?' I hesitated for a moment before I replied.

'Mr Webber has invited me to stay at Battle Tower until they return,' I said. 'It is not my wish, though.'

'You do not care for Battle Tower, then?' He glanced round at the beautiful, crowded banqueting room.

'It is not Battle Tower,' I said slowly. 'It is . . . '

'I understand perfectly,' said Charles. 'You will be staying here because people think it is better for you, but perhaps you are not altogether happy with the company you will be in?'

'I don't know the Webber family very well,' I said. 'And anyone else in the district is practically a stranger.'

'I'm not, I hope,' said Charles. 'My brother is in poor health, and we have no hostess at The Little Manor House. But occasionally my brother does have a dinner party, and invites his old friends — '

He broke off, and I thought of the conversation I had overheard at the engagement ball.

'Is your brother always in poor health?' I asked curiously. 'I mean — is he really ill?'

'Ill?' His voice was bitter. 'I suppose self-destruction is a form of illness. However, as Michael has practically destroyed everything, and sold his birthright, and squandered his inheritance, he can only destroy himself now. But he is my brother, and we are still the Ancrofts, and the door of every house in Northumberland is open to us. Our host is well aware of that. What

I am saying is, if we accept hospitality, we still return it. And while your father is away, we will see what can be arranged.'

Suddenly, despite all my mixed feelings of that day, I felt that I had one friend in the Border country. It was plain that he was going to make an effort to see me before long. I had the impression that a lot depended on how his brother was. Undoubtedly he was loyal to that brother, despite the fact that he had sold Battle Tower. At first I could not grasp the full significance of the rather peculiar relationship between the Webbers and the Ancrofts.

After a time, I realized that Mr Webber treated the Ancrofts with great respect. The best people in the county still visited The Little Manor House, when Michael Ancroft chose to entertain, and Mr Webber was eager to be on good terms with the two brothers. The fact that they accepted invitations to Battle Tower occasionally, and sometimes invited the Webbers to The Little

Manor House showed clearly their high standards and lack of pettiness. Nevertheless, beneath the well-bred exterior, I knew that Charles at all events felt very deeply about the loss of Battle Tower.

We were not able to talk together as long as we would have liked. There were speeches to be made; toasts to be drunk.

Mr Webber appeared to be very pleased at having so many people under his roof.

'I have prevailed upon some of our guests to stay on a few days,' he told me, when everyone seemed to be standing in chattering groups. 'Amelia's cousin, Miss Maxine Hart, is staying here with her parents. Maxine is only fifteen, I know, but she is quite a self-assured young lady for her age. She will be company for you during your father's absence.'

'Thank you,' I said. 'It is kind of you to be so concerned about my welfare.'

'It is a pleasure, Miss Hagan. Let me raise my glass in a toast to you — you are the most beautiful bridesmaid I have ever seen — or ever hope to see. A bridesmaid now; some day an even lovelier bride.'

'Thank you,' I murmured, but as I spoke an icy chill seemed to creep right through me; I could scarcely repress a shudder.

'Is Mrs Webber any better?' I enquired, wanting to take his attention off me.

He frowned slightly. 'I am afraid there is no hope of improvement now,' was the brief reply. I had never mentioned to anyone, not even Nellie, my unpleasant encounter with his wife.

My father and Amelia had driven over to Wild Witton to change and prepare for their journey. They called back at Battle Tower to say goodbye to everyone.

Amelia looked incredibly elegant in a wine-cloured outfit; my father was wearing grey, and looked gay and handsome. As he stooped to kiss me goodbye, I felt a terrible pang. I stood and waved my handkerchief until their carriage was out of sight. It was June now; the snow had long melted from the Cheviots, but despite the warm sun, the wind was cool. I shivered in my thin gown.

'You are cold, Miss Hagan,' said a solicitous voice at my elbow. It was Charles.

'Somebody walking over her grave, no doubt,' chimed in Herbert Webber, with his sly smile.

I felt instinctively that Charles no more liked Herbert Webber than I did. I moved to go back into the house. By now it was well into the afternoon; tea was being served. There was to be dancing in the evening, and a buffet supper instead of a hot meal. This was not surprising, in view of the banquet we had been given after the wedding.

In spite of feeling a bit lost somehow after seeing my father leave with his bride, yet there was a promise of excitement ahead; a promise of seeing more of Charles Ancroft.

Nellie helped me dress for the evening, sweeping my hair high on my head, as Cosette had shown her. Since I had known Amelia, I had acquired a number of new dresses. Some of these I'd had made, and she had helped me choose the styles. Others were gowns of hers, worn once or twice, or sometimes not at all, carefully altered to fit me by Nellie. Amelia said she saw no reason for me to go on wearing mourning for my great-uncle, particularly as we no longer lived in Ireland, and Papa agreed with her.

Nellie helped me into a new, amber-coloured ball gown, and I went down to join the other guests.

'I love dancing,' confided Maxine Hart. In pale green, with her auburn hair piled high, too, she looked a good deal older than her fifteen years, and she had the poise and assurance to go with it. 'Unfortunately, there are not as many *young* gentlemen here as I would like. It was a lovely wedding — when your father and Cousin Amelia return from their honeymoon, you must come and stay with us in Durham. We are not far from the town, really. You must see the cathedral — there are many places of interest.'

I was about to thank her for this kind invitation, when Charles appeared again.

'I'll book my usual two dances, Miss Hagan . . . and, of course, two with you, Miss Hart.'

Every so often, as the evening went on, I would think of Papa, married to Amelia. And then the dancing would start up again, and I would be whirled away in somebody's arms. Naturally, the arms I wanted to be in were Charles'. Already I was talking to him about Ireland, and my life at Dundreary House, and how Rory had died earlier that year. And he told me all about his life in the army, and also about his life when he had lived at Battle Tower. He told me, very briefly, that his brother had been married, but that his wife had run off with another man, and was living in France.

'Michael's whole personality seemed to undergo a change when that happened,' he said. I could tell that it was painful for him to talk about these things, and yet I was flattered that he felt able to confide in me on such a short acquaintanceship. He told me that he knew every stone and every tree in the grounds at Battle Tower.

'To the east of the long carriage-drive to the stables is a dense tangle of ancient trees and undergrowth dropping to a small, damp ravine. It's wild and uncultivated — we always called it The Wilderness. I used to play there a lot as a child.'

'I shall make a point of going there and looking at it,' I said.

'And further along, there is another place I used to play in; a tiny, derelict cottage. I suppose one of the game-keepers or someone lived in it at one time, but it's been empty ever since I can remember.'

'You are certainly the belle of the ball,' remarked Herbert Webber, when it was his turn to dance with me. 'Yes, indeed, Cousin Basil is well pleased with this day's work. Amelia married off and ensconced at Wild Witton with a well-connected Irish gentleman — and just for good measure, there is a beautiful daughter thrown in. The unfortunate Mrs Lucy Webber grows daily more indisposed, but Basil bears it with remarkable fortitude. One cannot help admiring him.'

The laugh which followed this remark had an unpleasantly cynical sound. 'Indeed, remarkable fortitude is shown on all sides. No doubt young Ancroft, your handsome soldier-boy, has been regaling you with the sad story of their lost home, money, land and so on. All Basil's now. But they turn up here with the rest of the Border families, gaping at the Chillingham bull, eyeing the chandeliers that were once theirs, and slyly touching the great, carved staircase, down which, no doubt, they would like to pitch the present owner.'

'Mr Webber,' I said coldly, 'are you sure you have not had too much to drink?'

I was not sure how to handle him, but the things he was saying were thoroughly distasteful.

'Certainly I have had too much to drink,' he replied, quite unabashed. 'And why not, on such an occasion? The wedding of my sister-in-law — or does she cease to be my sister-in-law now that she is married again? Dear me, I hadn't thought of that . . . instead, she becomes your mother — think of that, Miss Hagan — your mother!'

I found his company anything but pleasant, but politeness decreed that I could not refuse to dance with him. Nor could I refuse Basil Webber, whose large hands held me just a shade more tightly than I liked, as we waltzed together.

'I want you to enjoy every minute of your stay here,' he remarked.

'That is very kind of you,' I replied.

He squeezed my hand, and I was

thankful I was wearing kid gloves.

In spite of the fact that I did not care for the Webbers, though, I found that I did enjoy myself very much while Papa and Amelia were away. We attended several functions in the neighbourhood, including a dinner party at The Little Manor House. Nellie dressed me with special care for that; she remarked that Lieutenant Charles Ancroft was a very nice young gentleman.

'I know you like him,' she said, smiling, 'And when you think they once lived here . . . what a shame, Miss Maura.'

Herbert Webber came with us, but not his mother. She frequently declined invitations, pleading ill-health. Charles and Michael received us graciously. During one of our conversations, Charles had told me that Michael was the son of his father's first marriage, and that he himself had been born when Michael was approaching twenty. So they were really only half-brothers, which probably accounted for the dissimilarity in their looks.

The Little Manor House, although shabby outside, and small by Battle Tower standards, was well appointed within. It was plain that the most precious possessions, the family portraits and the treasured pieces of silver and china, had been brought here. Likewise, a handful of faithful servants remained in their service. Observing Michael at close quarters, I could see that he was a sick, unhappy man. Charles was fond of him, I knew that, and I knew that he would be loyal to him to the end.

Probably with an understanding wife at the back of him, things would have been different for Michael. But his wife had betrayed him, and the seeds of self-destruction which were within him, had burst into flower. Although he was charming that evening, I noticed that his glass was filled again and again throughout dinner, and that his hands trembled when he held anything.

Charles was attentive to all his guests,

but when his eyes met mine, I felt that I was the only one there whose presence he really cared about. This, despite the fact that Maxine Hart chattered to him a great deal at the dinner table.

She was certainly a pert and forward miss for fifteen years, but she was gay and jolly, and she brightened up the Webber household. With surprising quickness the days passed, and then the honeymooners returned, happy and excited, and laden with gifts for everyone.

Amelia's kiss was no less warm than Papa's when she greeted me. She had bought a fur cape and some bonnets in Paris, also shoes, jewellery, and endless little things which had taken her fancy. She had bought me some very stylish boots.

'I hope they fit. I know your size, but it's always a risk.' They fitted perfectly, and I was delighted with them.

As mistress of Wild Witton, Amelia began to entertain quite lavishly. Papa fell in with her wishes, although I had a feeling sometimes that he would have preferred a quieter life. He liked to read; he enjoyed riding and shooting and fishing; he enjoyed company too, up to a point, but not the endless round of social activities which Amelia considered essential.

That summer before I started school, because of my step-mother's keenness to entertain, I saw quite a lot of Charles. He was still stationed nearby, although he said he was shortly to be posted farther away. Amelia organized picnics, balls, parties, and whist drives. As well as tennis, we played croquet, sometimes until long after midnight. Indeed, on one such occasion we played croquet until three o'clock in the morning, servants holding candles over the hoops as we aimed at them.

In late August, just before I started school, there was a shooting party at Battle Tower. Charles was not there, having been posted to the south of England. He said that he hoped to see me at Christmas. In my heart, I wished that we could have written to each other, but I knew that at Byrne Lodge School where I was to go, such things would not be permitted. He shook my hand very warmly on the last occasion I saw him, and said he hoped I would enjoy school.

I went out with the shooting party at Battle Tower. Basil Webber was an expert shot, as was his cousin, Herbert, despite his physical disabilities. In fact, all the men were, not least my father, who loved the sport. The cries of the beaters; the whirr of wings, gunfire, and birds dropping out of the cloudless sky; it had an almost hypnotic effect on me.

Then the luncheon brake would appear, and a hot meal would be served outside. The guests were all older than I was; I wished with all my heart that Charles had been there. This I confided to Nellie, and she agreed it was a bit dull for anyone my age.

Just before we returned to Wild Witton, I explored the place which Charles had told me they called The

Wilderness. I also walked on and found the tumbledown little cottage, half hidden by trees. It made me feel closer to him.

I walked back across the parkland in front of the house. It was beautiful, with its dark tunnels of yews, mossy urns and statues, and borders blazing with a hotchpotch of colour. Beyond the shaven lawn, the bell-shaped trees were fired gold by the late afternoon sun.

Basil Webber seemed to appear from nowhere, and he was alone, too, which was unusual when he had guests. 'My dear Miss Hagan!' he exclaimed. 'I trust you are not lonely, taking a walk by yourself. I have been so busy with my other guests — have I neglected you?'

'Not at all,' I replied. 'I am enjoying a stroll by myself.'

'You like the grounds? You like Battle Tower?' His eyes were running over me, as if my reply was very important.

'Well, yes, naturally,' I said. His pride in the place was almost fanatical, and yet, neither he nor any of the other

Webbers seemed to belong there.

'You will be going to school shortly. Are you happy about that?'

'I am a trifle nervous. I have never been away from home before, and it was a big wrench leaving Ireland.'

He nodded his head understandingly as he walked along beside me, almost imperceptibly moving closer. I knew instinctively that he wanted to touch me; to make some form of caress. He resisted the temptation, but I knew the desire was there.

The curious mixture of revulsion and fear which this man roused in me rose up. I quickened my footsteps in the direction of the house, and he fell into step beside me. Perhaps he sensed my unease, as he began to talk casually about the hunting season, and horses. He also asked how Josty was faring, the chestnut mare he had insisted on giving me. Even so, I felt a sense of relief when we joined the other guests.

7

Byrne Lodge School was a secluded red brick building set in a tiny village about six miles from the sea. The nearest town was Scarborough. Papa and Amelia travelled there with me, and Mrs Chorley, the lady who ran it, greeted us kindly.

She was stout and middle-aged, but she had a lively mind. We were given afternoon tea in her sitting room, which was very comfortable, with a cheerful fire crackling in the hearth.

'You sound as if you have had a good grounding in most subjects,' said Mrs Chorley, to me. 'Perhaps a little specialization in music and dancing. Elocution, deportment, French — we are very keen on those subjects here. We also teach our girls how to run an establishment — how to deal with servants — and how household accounts should be kept.'

After tea she showed us round the house. In one room, two girls sat playing a duet on the piano. In another, a tall pleasant-faced woman was giving a French lesson to a group of girls in white blouses and navy blue skirts. This was how Mrs Chorley preferred her pupils to dress during lesson times.

'And this is where you will sleep, Miss Hagan. You will be sharing a room with Miss Phyllis Astley, and Miss Cassia Addy. All the girls sleep three in a room.'

I looked at the three narrow white beds with lockers, and the three single wardrobes. Everything at Byrne Lodge was plain but comfortable. A sturdy tree was growing outside the window, and below was a pleasant, spacious garden. It was very private.

Some time later, Papa and Amelia kissed me goodbye, and went to Scarborough, where they were spending the night in an hotel. My trunk had been carried up to my room by the manservant, Henry, and I met my room-mates for the first time. They were changing into pretty blouses for the evening meal.

Phyllis Astley was a quietly spoken, neat looking girl. She was tall and thin, even perhaps a trifle gawky, but she had nice grey eyes and a kind smile. Cassia was quite breathtakingly lovely. She had black hair escaping in little curly tendrils around her heart-shaped face, a very pink and white complexion, and small teeth that looked like seed pearls when she smiled.

She put on the loveliest cream silk and lace blouse. 'So you're from Ireland,' she said. 'I've been there — I've been to several house parties there. I like Ireland — but to visit, not to live there.'

She laughed infectiously, and chattered on, saying that we had to act as each other's maids, there being no lady's maids at the school.

'*And* we have to do all our own mending, too.' She grimaced, and then gave Phyllis an affectionate squeeze

'But Phyllis often does mine. Aren't I lucky?'

'Yes, you are,' said Phyllis. 'Soon, Miss Hagan, you will realize how completely selfish, frivolous, unreliable, shallow and fickle your other room-mate is.'

'And vain. Don't forget that,' put in Cassia, admiring herself in the mirror.

'And vain, to the exclusion of all else.'

Cassia nodded approvingly. 'Thank goodness she's told you the worst,' she said, with an impish smile. 'Now I don't have to pretend to be otherwise, which I might have done, for at least a week. Angel Phyllis, will you fasten my blouse at the back?'

Suddenly, to my surprise I began to feel at home with these two girls, and found myself telling them about my life in Ireland, and about my father's marriage, which appeared to intrigue them greatly, particularly Cassia. As we were talking, the dinner gong sounded through the house.

'Come on, Cassia. You know how Mrs Chorley dislikes anyone being late,' said Phyllis.

We went down the wide, shallow staircase into the cheerful dining room. Several long tables were set out, all with white damask cloths and good flower arrangement. Floral art was taken very seriously at Byrne Lodge; there was a roster for flower arranging.

After dinner the girls did prep, and then read, embroidered, or played games until bedtime. I was not the only new girl there, and Miss Conway, a young and very jolly looking mistress introduced us all. For the older girls, which meant Cassia, Phyllis and myself, it was lights out at ten o'clock. I was tired, but the excitement of the day, and the strangeness of the new life I was facing, made sleep difficult. Cassia chattered for a while in the darkness, and then I heard her breathing become deep and even. Phyllis was already asleep; the whole house was silent; it was then that I realized, perhaps for the first time, how very uprooted I felt. Leaving Dundreary; moving to England and Wild Witton; my father's marriage, and now coming away to school in Yorkshire. My bedroom, full of my familiar belongings, was far away. And so was Nellie. At last I fell asleep, but when I woke in the morning, my pillow was damp. It was damp outside, too, with rain beating against the windows, giving the garden a depressingly wintry look.

That first day at Byrne Lodge seemed very long. We had prayers in the Hall, then breakfast, and then I was enrolled for various studies under different teachers. My German was praised, but not my French, and Madame D'arcie was entrusted with improving it. Mrs Chorley was strict, but not too strict. She kept her pupils busy, but they had leisure time as well. She wanted to give the girls the tuition which she considered necessary for a lady; to imbue them with any social graces they may have lacked, and, quite simply, to give their parents value for the high fees they were paying her.

I was soon writing home, and receiving letters from Papa, and sometimes Amelia, and always a faithful, regularly weekly letter from Nellie.

'Is your father very rich?' enquired Phyllis, when I had been there a few weeks. We were in the bedroom together one evening. Cassia was having a music lesson.

'Papa? I don't really know . . . ' I paused. 'I suppose he's not really very rich.'

'I have no father,' said Phyllis. 'We are not rich at all. My uncle pays my fees here.'

'Oh,' I said, not really knowing how to reply.

'No doubt you have been brought up to think it is just a little vulgar to discuss money?'

'Money isn't everything,' I said uneasily.

'No? It can buy everything, though.'

Phyllis picked up a blouse of Cassia's

that was thrown carelessly over the bed. 'This one blouse cost more than everything I have put together.'

'Cassia is rich, then?'

'Very. She brought jewellery here the first term, but Mrs Chorley locked it away, and wouldn't allow her to wear it. She is always trying to keep Cassia down. Her clothes are beautiful, though. Her stays are made in Paris!'

This brief conversation made me see my room-mates in a different light. 'She is dreadfully spoilt, of course. And when we go for walks she looks up and smiles if there are any young gentlemen about. Mrs Chorley gets very vexed indeed. Undoubtedly Cassia will make a good match as soon as possible.'

A good match — where had I heard those words before?

I remembered then. Mr Webber had said Papa would want me to make one.

'If one is rich, one has a very good chance of making a good match,' went on Phyllis. 'Yet if you are poor, you *need* to marry money. Life is very unfair, I suppose. Mrs Chorley says she educates us to be good wives, whether our husbands are rich or poor. But I know she considers it a big feather in her cap if one of her ex-pupils makes a brilliant match. That is the whole idea behind this school.'

For a moment I was too surprised to speak. Phyllis sat in front of the mirror, and pinched some colour into her pale cheeks.

'I shall probably be an old maid — ' she began, when the door opened, and in came Cassia.

'I suppose you two are talking about me?'

'Who else? I've been telling Maura how fabulously wealthy you are — and how you can afford to leave expensive blouses lying around — and how you have French perfume, which you daren't use with Mrs Chorley around — and how your stays are made in Paris — '

'And that's not all! I have an admirer — a subaltern who is spending some leave with an aunt in Scarborough. He's going to call, and say he is my cousin!'

'Cassia!' Phyllis' eyes were wide with shock. 'He can't! Mrs Chorley would write to your parents to check up — you would be discovered in no time. And then where would you be?'

'Oh well . . . ' Cassia was quite unabashed. 'Anyway, he's going to write to me at the village post office, and give me his address in Scarborough. I plan to meet him somehow.'

Our conversation about money was speedily forgotten as we listened to Cassia's daring plans concerning her admirer. With some difficulty they corresponded, and managed a brief, fleeting rendezvous, aided somewhat nervously by Phyllis and me. I knew we were breaking all the rules of the school, and I had many a battle with my conscience, but I was at an age when I was easily influenced by others. And as Nellie would have put it, Cassia could have charmed a duck off a lake.

Shortly before we broke up for the Christmas holidays, I had a letter from

Papa telling me that Mr Webber's wife had died. I could not help feeling that there would be a sense of relief at Battle Tower.

One night, Cassia, Phyllis and I were in our bedroom preparing for bed. We were just about to extinguish the candle when there was a noise at the window.

'What's that?' asked Phyllis, clutching her wrapper round her. We sat on our beds, looking at each other. All was quiet, then came the sound of something against the window. Cassia rose, drew back the blind, and held the candle there, looking out. There was another patter on the glass, and she gave a little cry. Then she lifted up the sash, and looked down.

'Oh!' she gasped. 'Oh!'

'What's going on?' asked Phyllis. 'What is it, Cassia?' Cassia turned and faced us.

'It's Roger,' she said. 'He's climbing up the tree.'

'Never!' gasped Phyllis. 'You must stop him, Cassia! He might fall — and we'll all get into awful trouble anyway, if he's caught.'

A delicious thrill of fear ran through me as I sat on the bed. In spite of the danger we were all in, as the prudent Phyllis kept reminding us, it was certainly exciting. Although Charles and I could not correspond, I still thought about him frequently, and I was hoping he would be home on leave at Christmas. I couldn't help thinking how wonderful it would be to have *him* climbing up the tree to see me.

'He's coming — he won't be long now,' said Cassia.

'But what's he going to do when he *does* come?' Phyllis looked distracted with anxiety.

No reply from Cassia, just a swish from her expensive wrapper as she peered out into the darkness. It was chilly in the bedroom; I shivered, but as much from pleasurable anticipation as from anything else. After a while we heard Cassia speaking in a low voice; there was the faint sound of a man's voice replying.

She turned and faced us again. 'He's going to climb through the window,' she said. 'He's been recalled from leave by his regiment. I think he's going abroad somewhere.'

I clasped my hands with excitement. Phyllis was speechless. Cassia opened the sash as high at it would go. 'Hold me, girls,' she commanded.

Phyllis held her round the waist, and I held Phyllis' waist; apparently that was not right, though. Cassia took the top sheet off her bed, and knotted it several times round the bedpost.

'See the knot doesn't slip,' she said over her shoulder, and lowered the sheet through the window. The next moment a man's figure appeared on the ledge; long legs dangled over, and finally slid onto the floor.

'Good evening, ladies. Please excuse me,' he said, wiping his hands on his handkerchief.

Cassia introduced us. His name was Roger West.

'At your service.' He bowed in our

direction, and clicked his heels very smartly. He was not in uniform, but was wearing a well cut dark suit. He was a handsome young man, with a fine, military bearing, and thick, wavy brown hair. He seemed very upset, though. His eyes turned back to Cassia.

'I had to come! I don't know when I may see you again . . . oh, dearest Miss Addy — '

'Hush!' Phyllis raised a warning finger. There were no locks on the doors of our bedrooms, which made this escapade doubly hazardous. The young man's voice dropped to a whisper.

'Dearest! Dearest! I cannot bear the thought of leaving you.'

It was like eavesdropping. Phyllis and I were witnessing a scene which should have been private, but one of the people concerned was so desperate about the situation that he seemed almost oblivious of our presence. With one accord Phyllis and I turned our backs; not without some reluctance on my part, and I expect on hers, too. I knew that they were locked in an embrace. I could hear the sound of heavy breathing, of whispers, and a faint sob from Cassia.

'My darling, I can't live without you. Can you — will you wait for me?'

'Oh, Roger . . . '

Dreams, promises, hopes; murmured words of endearment exchanged in a candlelit bedroom, with two pairs of ears listening.

I reflected that he must have asked Cassia where her room was, and she must have told him about the beech tree. If he were caught he would be in the most appalling trouble, and so would Cassia. Undoubtedly she would be expelled. But Phyllis and I might be as well!

'You must go now, I'm afraid, Mr — er —West,' said Phyllis, whose mind was evidently running on similar lines. 'Cassia would have to leave school immediately if anyone found out about this. And you have the task of climbing down before you.'

'Yes, of course. I do beg your pardon,

ladies. Please forgive me. I'll go now.'

We turned round. Cassia's hair was dishevelled, and still more alarming, the two top buttons of her wrapper had been undone. At the window, her ardent suitor again drew her to him, and kissed her with murmured endearments, before seizing the sheet, and lowering himself down. Cassia stood at the window, watching his descent. After what seemed an age, she waved her hand in the light of the candle, and closed the window.

'Well,' said Phyllis, when the curtains were drawn again — 'such behaviour, Cassia. It's quite outrageous — and look at that sheet, all twisted up — and with marks on — '

'Oh, I'll say I had a bad dream and fell out of bed. Leave me alone.'

Cassia made the bed again, and I could she was in tears.

'I'm sorry,' whispered Phyllis. 'It's bad luck, him being posted abroad. Do you really care for him, Cassia?'

'What difference does it make if I

do?' was the reply. 'What's the use, anyway? He's as poor as a church mouse. Papa would never consider it — never. He had better go to Afghanistan or wherever it is, and forget.'

She extinguished the candle, and we climbed into our beds. But for a long time she wept quietly into her pillow.

8

Christmas at Wild Witton was a very festive affair indeed. From the letters Nellie had written me, I gathered that life was quite hectic in comparison with the old days at Dundreary.

Trips to London, trips to Paris, parties, balls, and many other social functions were a feature of life at Wild Witton. Amelia liked a 'full house' as she described it.

She certainly had one over Christmas. We had the Webbers visiting, the Harts from Durham, and several other families who lived in the neighbourhood. Also visiting with the Harts was a Mr Albert Andrews, a man of about five-and-thirty, who had recently returned to England after many years abroad.

But best of all, Charles Ancroft was home on leave for Christmas. He had brought an army friend back with him, a young man called Kenneth Miles. Like Charles he was a Second Lieutenant; a pleasant-faced young man with a cheerful manner.

For part of the Christmas holidays Phyllis was coming from Manchester to stay with me, and we were both looking forward to it very much. The weather turned extremely cold, and the lake in the grounds at Wild Witton froze. Amelia was delighted, and planned a skating party, to be followed by a ball in the evening. Phyllis had arrived, and was entranced by everything.

'Oh, what a lovely place! You are lucky, Maura. It's beautiful.' She spoke wistfully.

'Wild Witton? Why, it's nothing beside Dundreary House in Ireland,' I said. But I had to admit that snow-covered, and set against the wintry beauty of parkland and lake, Wild Witton *did* look impressive.

Mr Webber, although in mourning, did not appear to be grief stricken, nor apparently was he foregoing any social pleasures because of his bereavement. Out of politeness I gave him my condolences, which he received in a very matter-of-fact way.

Charles shook my hand warmly. 'How well you look, Miss Hagan. I'm glad I could get Christmas leave.'

I could feel myself blushing; for a moment I was tongue-tied. It made me realize how very much I had looked forward to seeing him again.

There was so much company in the house, and so many guests to entertain, that I never got the chance to have a really long, private talk with Papa. He seemed pleased that I looked so well, and that I was happy at Byrne Lodge. Both he and Amelia went out of their way to make Phyllis' visit enjoyable.

Despite the cold, we had the most wonderful time skating. I was quite proficient at it; so were Papa and Amelia. Maxine Hart was an excellent skater, as were both the Webbers.

Mr Andrews and Amelia paired up, and went off with crossed hands;

Maxine seized my father and whirled away with him, and with one accord, Charles and I followed suit, and so did his friend with Phyllis.

The clasp of Charles' hands in mine, the sense of speed and the cold air stinging my cheeks gave me a feeling of exhilaration, and filled me with a wild happiness. We said very little, really, somehow the past months when we had not seen each other seemed to melt away. There was a feeling of companionship, of closeness; something indefinable between us, but something which we both felt.

We skated until the leaden sky began to send down thick flakes of snow again, and then, with much regretful laughter, we removed our skates, and our party headed for the house again.

We were giving a ball that night, but Phyllis, colouring up, had admitted to having no suitable gown.

'My stepmother has lots of clothes which she never wears. She will be only too pleased to help you out.'

'I couldn't possibly accept anything, Maura.'

'Don't spoil your stay by being like that, Phyllis. Amelia would never let you, anyway. She couldn't bear to have a guest here not enjoying themselves.'

This was true, and nothing pleased Amelia more than to go through her large wardrobe, with Cosette in attendance, while she flung gowns onto the bed in front of someone's admiring eyes. She soon had a cream-coloured gown altered for Phyllis, who looked very nice in it, despite her somewhat mousy brown hair, and sharp features.

Cosette and Nellie got us ready between them. I was in a pale lilac gown, wearing a pair of amethyst earrings which had been my mother's.

'Ah, the charming Miss Hagan,' said a voice at my elbow, when we were all assembled in the holly-bedecked hall, waiting for the dancing to begin. I turned round. It was Basil Webber.

'I must book my dances before the rush starts,' he said, smiling. 'No doubt

119

you and your school friend can hardly wait for the dancing to begin. Being away at school has been beneficial, I think . . . for you, I mean. Besides coming home looking even lovelier, there is a new sort of maturity about you.'

'Thank you, sir,' I said, rather distantly. Why did he make these curiously disconcerting remarks? Apart from anything else, I thought them in very bad taste, considering his recent bereavement. He booked dances with Phyllis as well as me, but I had a feeling that he was not in the least interested in dancing with her; that it was merely for the sake of appearances.

Michael Ancroft was not there. Charles told me briefly that his brother was not well at all. I sensed that he was worried about this, but he did not dwell on it. Instead, he asked me all about school, and indeed, all about everything that had happened since we had last met.

Far from being tongue-tied now, I found myself chattering away about all sorts of things. Phyllis was enjoying herself enormously, too, in her borrowed gown. I knew that Amelia would insist on her keeping it, which in fact she did.

And then Basil Webber claimed his dance. 'I have been looking forward to seeing you again,' he said. 'You must make the most of the time you are at home, to see your friends.'

I could not think of him as a friend, although it was plain that he wanted me to. Phyllis was sharing my room during her stay; not because it was necessary, but because we preferred it that way.

'That Mr Webber — ' she said, when we were both in our nightdresses.

'Which one?' I asked.

'The older one — the one whose wife recently died — he does look at you in the oddest way, Maura.'

'Yes,' I replied. 'He does.'

'He was telling me all about Battle Tower — he says we will be visiting there before the holidays end. Is he very rich?'

'Yes, I believe he is,' I said.

'Do you know, all the time he was dancing with me, Maura, he was asking questions about you?'

'Oh, was he?' I climbed into bed after Phyllis. 'What sort of questions?'

'All sorts, really. But mostly questions about what you are like at school, and what you are good at, and things like that.'

'Indeed?' Sudden annoyance shot through my tiredness. 'I hope you didn't tell him much, then.'

'I didn't. I knew you wouldn't wish it. Goodnight.'

Phyllis turned over and slept. I was overtired, and for a while sleep would not come. I had enjoyed the evening immensely, mainly due to Charles' presence, of course. Not so pleasant was the memory of Mr Webber; of the pressure of his hands, and the curiously searching gaze of his small eyes.

★   ★   ★

When Charles was due back from his Christmas leave, he and his friend, Kenneth, came to make their farewells to us at Wild Witton. Charles' face was pale and set. We had tea in the drawing room. Amelia was charming, and Papa was enjoying talking to the two young men, and yet I felt sad. After a while Charles mentioned that they were expecting to be posted to Gibraltar. I tried not to show my feelings. Our eyes met, and his were asking the same question as I was thinking — when would we see each other again? We could not put our thoughts into words, though. In the presence of others, we shook hands and said goodbye.

Fortunately I was not able to brood too much, as I had been invited back to Phyllis' house for a visit. I was astonished to find how modest her home was on the outskirts of Manchester. How strange to live in a small brick house, with but a maidservant, a cook, and a daily help. And yet, I enjoyed it. Phyllis' mother was kind, and very eager to make me feel welcome. For the first time, though, I realized what it meant to be poor. Not poor as people were in Ireland, or for that matter, in England. But to have as Phyllis had, education and a love of the beautiful; to want the best things in life, and yet to be wretchedly poor in comparison with most of the other girls at school.

And it was no less easy for her mother, brought up in fairly comfortable circumstances, but now leading a penny-pinching life as a poor widow. Going to bed that first night as Phyllis', I looked round at the threadbare carpet in the room, and the faded curtains. No wonder she did not envisage a very exciting future for herself.

'You see how differently we live here,' said Phyllis, a wry smile on her face. 'If I had the chance to marry a rich man — ' She paused.

'Yes? If you had the chance?'

'Then I would marry him.'

'Any man?' I asked, unpinning my hair.

'Within reason. Any man.'

'Even if he were old?'

'Even if he were old.'

'*I* wouldn't.'

'You say that, Maura, because you are not poor. You will have the chance to marry money in any case. Someone who is not only rich, but handsome and charming, I have no doubt.'

'Oh, Phyllis, you paint such a gloomy picture of yourself. Why should you not marry someone who is rich, handsome and charming?'

'Because I am poor and plain into the bargain. If I looked like Cassia — or like you for that matter — or alternatively, if I had money — things would be different. But when one is both poor and plain — '

'You mean if you had the chance you would marry — say — Mr Webber?' I don't know what made me say that.

'Yes, I would marry Mr Webber. But I will not have the chance — '

I sat brushing my hair without speaking for a moment.

'I would rather die!' I said, putting down my brush.

'Ah, you say that.' In the light of the oil lamp, a bitter little smile twisted Phyllis' mouth. 'If you had to choose between poverty and Mr Webber, you would choose Mr Webber.'

'But what about love?' I cried.

'What about it? If one stays single, one must do without it in any case.'

There seemed to be no arguing against Phyllis' reasoning. She kissed me good-night, and I lay for a long time thinking about what she had said.

9

Back at school, we exchanged chit-chat about our Christmas holidays, and settled down somewhat reluctantly at first for another term's work. I received the usual letters from home, and wrote the usual ones back. According to Nellie, the endless round of gaiety was still going on at Wild Witton. And then, one day when it seemed the winter would surely be drawing to a close, Mrs Chorley sent for me when I was halfway through a French lesson.

I tapped on the door of her room, and entered. She was seated at her desk, her face grave. She rose and came up to me straight away.

'Maura, my dear,' she said, putting her hand on my arm, 'you must try to be brave. You are wanted home at once. It is your father — ' She broke off.

'Papa!' I looked at her in an

uncomprehending, speechless horror.

'A shooting accident . . . try to be brave, Maura . . . '

From what seemed a long way off her voice came, consoling, comforting, trying to cushion the blow — the terrible knowledge that my father had accidentally shot himself, and that he was gravely ill.

* * *

There was no gaiety at Wild Witton now. People spoke in hushed voices; Amelia was paler than usual, but outwardly composed. No one appeared to know quite how the accident had occurred, but it had been at a shooting party at Battle Tower. I tip-toed into my father's darkened room.

How strange, how frightening it was to see him lying there, his head bandaged, his eyes closed. He had lain unconscious ever since the shooting; strangely, I had only been in the house a few hours before he regained consciousness, and recognized me.

'Maura!' he whispered hoarsely, ' . . . money, I have no money! What shall I do? They are wanting money from me . . . my child . . . what have I done to you?'

'Of course there is money, John,' said Amelia soothingly. I was startled at the hardness in her eyes when she turned to me, though. 'Now he has regained consciousness, perhaps we had better have the doctor straight away. Send someone for Dr Parnaby, Maura.'

Oddly enough, Papa did not seem to be aware of his wife's presence. I hurriedly despatched someone for the doctor, and at the same time a visitor was announced, Mr Basil Webber. I was bound to receive him, Amelia being still with my father.

'My dear Miss Hagan! This is such a dreadful business — how shocked you must be. I cannot tell you how sorry I am — if I can help in even the smallest way — '

Amelia had remarked how good he

had been, driving over almost every day to see how the patient was, and sending a groom over for news, if he was unable to come himself.

'Papa has regained consciousness,' I told him. 'He has recognized me.'

'Ah, that is splendid news.'

'We have just sent for Dr Parnaby — '

At this point Amelia came hurriedly into the room.

'Uncle Basil!' she cried. 'I saw your carriage driving up — John is conscious, and he is asking for you! Please come to him now ... and you, of course, Maura.'

The three of us went back to the sick-room. Looking down at my father's face in the semi-darkness, I longed to send the other two away, and have him to myself.

'Maura.' Again the beloved voice murmured my name. 'I have no money ... there is no money ... what shall I do? ... Webber ... there is no money.'

These were the tortured words which he repeated over and over again. His bemused, tormented brain seemed incapable of any other thought, except that there was no money. He still did not mention Amelia's name.

'Well, tell me all about it, then,' said Mr Webber quietly. 'Pray don't get so upset, or we shall be in trouble with the doctor. If there is anything of a financial nature worrying you, and you feel you must talk about it — well, what are friends for? Perhaps you would prefer the ladies to leave us so that we can talk man to man.'

I could not be quite sure, but Papa appeared to nod his assent.

'Just leave us together for a few minutes,' said Mr Webber in a low voice. 'I can put his mind at rest if he is having imaginary fears of this nature.'

I bent and kissed Papa's forehead; after a slight hesitation, Amelia did the same, and we left the two men alone.

We ordered tea for three in the library.

'Isn't it wonderful?' I said. 'Papa regaining consciousness, I mean.'

'Yes . . . oh, yes, of course. We must

not raise our hopes too high, I suppose.' Amelia looked thoughtful. 'I wonder what he meant, no money. You have never heard your father talk like that before, have you?'

'No — but then, surely, when people regain consciousness after a head injury — but it was in his chest that he shot himself wasn't it?'

'Yes, but he struck his head when he fell . . . I don't know all the details myself, Maura, and I don't think I want to. Perhaps Uncle Basil can throw some light onto why there is so much talk about money.'

Shortly afterwards the doctor arrived, and after taking tea with us, Mr Webber took his leave. He said he would be returning the next day, and that he was going to attend to some business matters for Papa. Another week passed, during which time my father's condition seemed to fluctuate between spells of unconsciousness, and uneasy consciousness, when he would talk about money, and ask for me, and then for Mr

Webber; never for Amelia.

Mr Webber was a constant visitor at Wild Witton. He seemed to spend hours closeted in Papa's study, going through his private papers and files. Indeed, at Amelia's request, he agreed to stay at Wild Witton for the time being, as Papa sometimes asked for him when he regained consciousness.

I did not care for the way Basil Webber appeared to take control of my father's affairs, but as Amelia approved, there was nothing I could do. And then, one afternoon, Mr Webber, Amelia, and a man who had been one of our house guests at Christmas, Mr Andrews, spent a long time in Papa's study. Amelia had told me at our house party that she and Albert Andrews had known each other years before, when they had both lived in Durham. As a boy, he had been considered a bit 'wild', and had gone to the colonies, where apparently he had done extremely well.

He was a handsome man, in a slightly florid way; I recalled them skating together at Christmas. But what was he doing here now? What were the three of them doing in Papa's study?

Later that evening, I knew.

'Well — er — Maura — ' began Mr Webber, using my Christian name for the first time. Mr Andrews had discreetly left the house; I had heard he was staying at Battle Tower.

'Well — er — this is a bad business, I'm afraid. Your father — well — '

'Your father has nothing — nothing!' cried Amelia. 'If anything happens to him, there is no will, but it doesn't make much difference anyway. I would be left with nothing — just a mountain of debts! I should have known better — he's just a shiftless Irishman — '

Blazing indignation and anger rose in me at her words. 'My father spent plenty on you,' I said contemptuously. 'Having money spent on you is all you care about — '

'Maura!' interposed Mr Webber. 'You mustn't speak to your stepmother like that. Things are bad enough for her — '

'Then she had better go back and live at Battle Tower,' I said bitterly. '*I'll* nurse Papa back to health — we can manage very well between us.'

'You've overlooked the fact that there is no money,' said Amelia bitingly. '*You* have nothing either — you're a pauper in this house.'

'Then Papa can sell the house when he is better,' I cried. 'We will get a smaller establishment.'

'Impossible, I'm afraid,' said Mr Webber. 'You see, I merely leased Wild Witton to your father . . . he talked of buying at a later date. He is being dunned for money from a number of people, and this is what is preying on his mind — '

Suddenly I could not bear to hear any more. I ran from the room. I wanted to summon Nellie as soon as possible. I wanted to sob out what I had been told, and for her to somehow comfort me. A feeling of unbelievable helplessness and insecurity swept over me. I was poor — poor — poor, like

Phyllis! I had no clear idea how all this had come about, but I knew that my unhappy father, hovering between life and death, had no peace of mind because of money worries.

And although Nellie's arms did comfort me that night, with the morning came the realization that I would have to face whatever there was to face.

'Maura, you look very pale. It is bright today, if cold. We were all a trifle upset last night; no doubt we can come to some arrangement about these money worries. Why not have a walk in the grounds with Mr Webber this morning?'

Amelia's voice was kind as she made this suggestion. I had no desire to walk in the grounds with Mr Webber, but under the circumstances, I could hardly refuse.

Warmly clad against the bitterness of the wind, we set off from the house together. I had slept little the night before. At first we walked along in silence, and it occurred to me that I had thought Wild Witton a poor place after our house in Ireland. Little had I known that it was merely leased — and from Mr Webber, of all people!

After a while he cleared his throat, and began to speak.

'Your father's condition does not alter much, my dear.'

I made no reply; indeed I could not trust myself to speak.

'You are so alone in the world,' he went on. 'Alone — and without means. And your poor father — '

'Don't!' I cried, my voice breaking. 'There is nothing I can do! I cannot make Papa well again — I cannot produce money to pay these debts — I can do nothing, nothing, to help him! And I would do anything.'

For a while my companion did not speak again. We were walking up to the highest point of the grounds surrounding Wild Witton. At the windswept summit, he took my arm, and pointed into the distance.

'What can you see over there?' he asked. To my surprise, from that position I could see Battle Tower.

'Why, Battle Tower,' I said.

He turned and looked at me, and I had a moment of intense illumination, accompanied by a fear so strong that I felt physically sick. I could feel the violent thump-thump of my heart; I had been hunted down at last.

'Battle Tower could be yours if you would share it with me.'

His large, strong hands closed over mine. 'If you marry me, Maura, there will be no more money worries. To me, your father's debts are nothing — nothing! Should he recover — for which we can only pray — I will see all is well for him. I could do it in such a way that he need never know. Yes, I know how proud these Irish gentlemen are . . . and should he not recover, I can still clear his debts now, and keep his name good. I will see he has the best of everything, and that your stepmother is provided for.'

He stood looking down at me.

'The world can be a harsh place for a

girl like you — a girl who has led a sheltered life; a young lady left virtually penniless. I would take care of you, Maura, if you marry me.'

It was not a romantic proposal by any means; just a reasoned argument that it would be a very wise thing if I were to marry him. I thought of Phyllis' words about marrying a rich man if she had the chance.

'But I don't love you!' I cried, finding my voice at last. I saw that a decision was being forced upon me; if I had a choice, what was it?

'What can you know of love? Just the romantic talk young ladies indulge in at school. You may feel you do not love me now, but after we are married you will grow to love me.'

'And you are so much older, Mr Webber.'

'My dear, you *need* an older man. Should your father recover — as we all hope he will — he will never be an active man again. His dearest wish, will, naturally, be to see his daughter settled with a close friend of his — a man he can trust. And as my wife, you could see your father as often as you wished — '

'Papa — ' I turned my head away to hide the tears.

'I will take care of you — and him.' Mr Webber's voice took on a persuasive urgency. 'I have already sent for a specialist from London to see him . . . and don't forget, you will have your nurse, or maid, whatever you like to call her — Nellie — isn't it? You will have her with you always. She practically brought you up, didn't she?'

I nodded without speaking. He was offering me a way out of my present desperate position. A specialist for my father; a permanent home for Nellie. Doubts and fears rose up in me — and — unbidden, the memory of Charles Ancroft's face. Some instinct deep inside me told me that I could not possibly marry this man. But if I did not marry him, what then?

'Mr Webber — ' I began, but he stopped me.

'Trust me, Maura. You will be happy as my wife. Much happier than you think now.' He raised my gloved hands to his lips and kissed them. I struggled against my dislike of contact with him.

'I may not be happy, and you may not be happy either,' I said.

'I shall be happy just to see you as mistress of Battle Tower. I shall ask nothing of you — nothing — only that you grace my house with your presence. Do not think about whether you love me or not — think of it as a new home for you and Nellie — a home where you can be secure. And also, you know your father will always have everything he needs.'

Put that way, my fears subsided. I was still confused; not sure. And yet, a home of my own, security, Nellie; he made everything sound so attractive.

I agreed to marry him. As we walked back to the house, the sound of screams came from a nearby copse, catching me unawares.

'Just some wild creature caught in a

141

snare,' remarked my future husband blandly. 'You are a country girl — you know how they scream and struggle when the trap springs.'

10

I sat with Nellie under the trees beside the lake in the grounds of Battle Tower. It was a hot June day; even so a slight breeze rustled the leaves overhead. My father had scarcely lingered for a week after I had given my promise to Mr Webber, despite the specialist who came post haste from London. Mr Webber told me that he would formally ask Papa's permission to marry me, and relieve his mind of financial worry at the same time.

This he did, but when I went in to see him afterwards, Papa had lapsed into unconsciousness again. Mr Webber said my father wanted the wedding to take place as soon as possible, and accordingly, plans were made. The specialist, an eminent man, stayed at Wild Witton, and had many consultations with Dr Parnaby, but only once did my father regain consciousness again, and ask for me.

'All is well, Papa,' I said soothingly, clasping his hands. 'Don't worry, Papa. All is well.'

The tears gushed unheeded down my cheeks; Amelia stood uneasily watching on.

'Maura — ' He struggled to speak. He did not look at Amelia, his blue eyes sought mine with a kind of desperate urgency; again he tried to say something, but the effort was too much. Minutes later Amelia pushed me out of the way, and closed his eyes, as if she could not bear to see the expression in them.

My wedding day seemed a long way off now. In fact, looking back, it scarcely seemed possible that it was me in that church, taking those solemn vows, wearing a purple costume as a token of mourning for Papa.

I could recollect the trembling inside me which would not stop; the peculiarly triumphant look on Amelia's face; the grim, set, look on Martha Webber's, and the unpleasant leer on the face of her son, who was best man.

Phyllis and Cassia were both there. Afterwards, when they kissed me, Cassia said nothing at all, but I saw understanding in her large, beautiful eyes. Phyllis smiled at me as though to say 'I told you so'. She gave me a quick squeeze.

'Never mind,' she said. 'I don't blame you one little bit, Maura. Stays made in Paris, from now on.'

I tried to smile. Afterwards it all seemed confused and unreal. The wedding breakfast, my grey travelling costume, and Nellie, quiet and attentive in the background . . . the beautiful fur cape my husband had bought me for a wedding gift . . . the journey to Dover . . . the bad crossing — and Paris.

Paris in springtime. I had never been before, and my new husband was pleased to show me everything he thought might interest and entertain me. Sometimes we dined at the hotel; sometimes he took me to famous and expensive restaurants. I was quite dazzled by the strange sights and smells.

I was impressed by the three-horsed omnibuses, by the self-possession of the Parisiennes; most of all by the women. They sat in the restaurants, richly attired in silks and velvets, plumes and flowers; in gowns stitched by toil-worn grisettes. They applied powder to their faces in public, and stared around in the boldest way imaginable.

My husband asked me to call him Basil, something which I did not find easy. Nevertheless, things were better than I had expected. This was largely due to the fact that he did not impose himself on me in any way. He had a separate room, and Nellie slept in the room which adjoined mine at the hotel. Gregory, my husband's valet, was also in Paris with us.

From time to time, my grief for my father still obtruded, but there were so many things to see and do, so many different sights to take in, that at night I was too tired to brood.

We spent a month in Paris. It was not

until we arrived back in Northumberland that there was a change in my husband's attitude. I had a magnificent room at Battle Tower. The fourposter bed was splendidly hung with white and gold brocade; the carpet was white, and the curtains were gold. The effect was one of brightness and sunshine.

'Isn't it beautiful?' exclaimed Nellie, unpacking my clothes. I looked through the window, at the great vista beyond. Another spring, and another new home. But this time it was to be a permanent one. My first dinner as mistress of Battle Tower was rendered somewhat gloomy by Mrs Webber, who complained that she was not feeling well.

Herbert said that I looked very well anyway, as befitted a new bride. 'Amelia is in Durham,' he went on, with a sly grin. 'Yes, indeed . . . she has kind friends in Durham — kind friends.'

His mother drew in her mouth disapprovingly. 'I cannot see that Amelia's affairs are of any interest to anyone in this house now,' she said.

'Amelia's affairs . . . ' said Herbert thoughtfully. He fingered his wineglass, the corners of his mouth curling in that smile I so hated. 'But surely, in some degree or another she appears to be related to all of us. She's my sister-in-law, and you, dear Mother, are her mother-in-law, by her first marriage, of course. By her second marriage, she became Maura's mother, and, presumably, she is now Basil's mother-in-law.'

He burst out laughing. I thought his remarks were in very bad taste; in any case, like his mother, I wanted no more of Amelia. Basil did not appear to mind, though. He remarked with a grin that he did not anticipate any interference from his mother-in-law, if mother-in-law she was.

Later, Mrs Webber and I withdrew, and left the two men smoking cigars and talking.

'Strange how things happen,' observed Mrs Webber, sniffing at some smelling salts. 'When you first came here to stay, I never dreamed you would ever come here as Basil's bride.'

'I did not either,' I said nervously.

'It's all been very sudden — very sudden indeed. You will find out my cousin can be a very difficult man in some ways. Very difficult.'

She made this remark with a peculiar sort of relish, and went on to say that she was glad he got on so well with her and Herbert.

'You have met the housekeeper, Mrs Reay. It will be to you she will come for instructions. I've never been mistress here officially, of course, although I've practically had to run the place . . . and Herbert acts as steward, here. I really don't know how Basil would do without us. But naturally, the idea of doing without us does not arise.'

I felt that she was telling me this to make certain things clear right from the start.

'You have a lot of things to learn about Basil,' she went on, an unpleasant smile hovering around her mouth. A feeling of repugnance rose within me, and it did not subside when we were joined by the two men. We sat playing cards for the rest of the evening.

That night, after Nellie had left me, I sat in my Paris bought lace-trimmed white satin wrapper, beside the coal fire in my bedroom. I was startled to hear a slight movement in the dressing room adjoining mine. There was a cough, and then the sound of a cupboard being closed. I stood up, the blood suddenly pounding in my head. I looked at the heavy door between the two rooms. There was a keyhole, but no key in it. I stood there, listening intently. It was quiet now. Then the door was opened abruptly, and my husband stood there in a dark blue dressing robe.

There was a fixed smile on his face. He closed the door behind him, and advanced towards me. 'You look surprised, my dear. Come, give me a kiss.'

He had kissed me before, in a fatherly sort of way. I had not enjoyed it, but I had borne with it as best I could. This time, though, he gripped me hard around the waist, and pressed his lips to mine in a long, intimate, disgusting kiss, which outraged me. I resisted him with all my strength, which, however, did not appear to upset him. He was holding me in a rigid embrace; as I bent my head backwards, his hungry mouth followed mine. Then, abruptly, he stopped kissing me, and held me in front of him. I was panting with fear and shock.

'You said — ' I gasped. 'You told me you would ask nothing of me — '

'I intended to have you for my wife,' he said coldly. 'I have always used any means at my disposal to get what I want. The end justifies the means.'

With a rough movement he pulled off my wrapper, leaving me in my white, lawn nightdress. My mouth went dry; I was unable to utter a sound.

'You've got a home, and Nellie,' he said. 'That's what you wanted, isn't it?'

'Yes, but . . . ' I began, through trembling lips.

'Then remember the vows you made

on your wedding day. And keep them. I can send your precious Nellie away any time I want. Just reflect on these things, and you will realize you are in no position to strike bargains with me. Now get into bed.'

He waited until I did so, and then extinguished the lamp.

★   ★   ★

In the weeks that followed, I tried to adjust myself to this new life. It was true that I had a home and Nellie; it was true that my father's debts had been cleared, but I had paid a high price for these things. Now I had all the time in the world to think back and regret. I had been tricked — yes, trapped, into this marriage — and yet, what else could I have done?

Circumstances had compelled me to marry this man; he himself had implied that it was no more than my plain duty to my father. And I had believed him when he had said he would ask nothing of me save that I would grace his house with my presence. I knew differently now.

I used to dread the nights, but I was fearful of offending him. Suppose he sent Nellie away? I had no money at all. That was a further humiliation; I was not given an allowance of any sort.

'You may have what clothes you want. I will help you to choose them,' he said.

If I wore jewellery it was carefully locked away afterwards, except for the one or two modest pieces which my mother had left. I could not have run away because I had no means at all to support myself and Nellie. Out of my husband's sight I shed bitter tears, and yet, there was nothing to be done. My life seemed over before it had begun. And Basil Webber soon made it clear that he did not want Phyllis or any of my school friends visiting at Battle Tower.

There was no need for me to tell Nellie how unhappy I was. Once she came into my room, and caught me weeping. I felt her gentle arms around me.

'Oh, Miss Maura, if only your father hadn't met that woman when he went to London . . . '

We clung together for a while without speaking.

'We have each other, Nellie,' I said bravely.

'Things will get better. You see, they'll get better, Miss Maura. Once you get used to — ' She broke off.

Can one get used to unhappiness? At that time, I did not believe so. At Battle Tower I always had the feeling that my movements were watched. The gimlet eyes of Martha Webber seemed to peer at me from unexpected places; the sly ones of her son followed me as I came and went. I knew that the fact that I was now mistress of Battle Tower did not please the other Mrs Webber. She had been very quick to let me know that she and Herbert were permanencies there, notwithstanding her cousin's second marriage to a perfectly healthy wife. Nevertheless, she was bound to hand over certain responsibilities to me, as mistress, and she dared do no other, because whatever she felt, she had no intention of risking offending Basil Webber. When we did not have company in the house, the four of us usually dined together, but we did not spend all our time in each other's company.

Martha Webber and her son never came into the blue drawing room, as it was called. There I spent many evenings alone with my husband. Often he would sit and play the piano while I embroidered. He had a private golf course, and kept a professional. He would talk about his form, while I sat listening with a mixture of dislike and boredom. Occasionally he would sit morosely, drinking whisky. I dreaded such evenings, because, although he never became actually drunk, the liquor roused all the coarseness in his nature. His fumbling hands and whisky-soaked breath filled me with disgust.

Amelia had dropped out of my life as quickly as she had come into it. She had assisted Basil Webber to gain the wife he wanted, and I had no doubt she had been adequately rewarded. She cared nothing for my happiness or anything else concerning me. Wild Witton was empty again. She had left the Border country, and was living in Durham, where the odious Herbert said she had 'kind friends'. I had no doubt who one of them was, at all events; Nellie had confirmed my suspicions regarding Amelia and Albert Andrews.

For the first few months after my marriage, I lapsed into a state approaching apathy. The shock of my father's death, bravely borne at first, now seemed worse than ever. Had it really been an accident when he shot himself? But if not, perhaps he had chosen what seemed to him the best course.

Looking at myself in the mirror, I thought with loathing of my husband's embraces, from which there seemed to be no escape.

And yet, although a part of me felt disgusted and defiled by being Basil Webber's wife, another part of me was completely untouched. I was still *me* inside; still Maura Hagan. Very occasionally, when we had guests to the house, Michael Ancroft would be there, looking very ill.

One evening he was among a number of gentlemen whom my husband was entertaining in the library. I retired to my room with a book, and became quite absorbed in it. It was late when Basil appeared; he had been drinking, and seemed in a talkative mood.

'Not in bed yet? Waiting up for me, were you?'

These were the sort of remarks which he enjoyed making, and to which I never replied.

'Well, I suppose you remember young Ancroft, don't you?' he went on. I felt myself flushing; growing tense.

'Yes, of course you do. Gallantly stopped our runaway horses, didn't he? And you enjoyed dancing with him

— well, it appears he caught a fever of some sort in Gibraltar. He's on his way home. He'll be having some leave to get over it.'

'Oh,' I said, half in relief.

'He's quite a favourite with the young ladies, I gather. He'll be setting some hearts a-flutter while he's on sick leave, I've no doubt. Not so Michael — he's had his fill of women with that wife of his. Led him a dance by all accounts — ran away with another man in the end — yes, and took what she could with her, too. He was a fool with her, and what good did it do him? Your father was a fool too, my dear.'

'How dare you say that about Papa?' I cried, stung to a retort at last.

'It's the truth — and you know it. He gratified Amelia's every whim — and where did it get him? She made a fool of him, that's all. No woman has ever made a fool of me.'

He pulled me roughly towards him. 'I'm just letting you know this, in case you should ever be tempted to try.'

11

The morning following that conversation, I woke early, and lay in bed quietly, lest I disturb my husband. I had thought about my circumstances before, with a kind of hopeless resignation, but now other ideas began to stir within me. I would make my life as bearable as possible, but I would have to use guile to do that. I wanted more freedom — I *intended* to have more freedom, but I would have to tread carefully.

I would have to feign an affection which I did not feel. The idea was loathsome, and yet, there was no other way.

'Basil, I think I could do some good if I went into the village of Witton, and gave some help to the poor there. I used to do this when I lived in Dundreary with Papa.'

I mentioned this the following evening, when we were together in the blue drawing room. My husband was looking at a magazine about field sports. He lowered it, and fixed his small, keen eyes on me. I laughed.

'Don't look at me like that,' I said. 'I know there *are* poor people in Witton — and sick people, too. Surely it would please you for your wife to do some charitable work.'

The idea did not appear to displease him. He rubbed his chin, and looked thoughtful.

'You really want to do something like that, Maura?'

'Of course,' I said. 'If I am living here, then surely you want me to take an interest in everything? Now that you have a young and healthy wife, don't you think she should be seen playing her part as mistress of Battle Tower?'

'Ah, so you are beginning to realize the advantages of your position.' He put down the magazine. 'Come and sit beside me, and we'll talk about it.'

I did so, and before we retired, he agreed that while he was playing golf, or occupied in some pursuit that I didn't share, it would be a good thing for me to visit the poor and needy in Witton.

We had our own pew at the village church; lists were kept of those who were sick and in trouble, and there was always work for willing hands. Naturally, I would be driven to and from any visits by Bywell, the coachman, and accompanied by Nellie.

'I don't suppose Martha will be interested in joining you on your errands of mercy. Still, you had better ask her about it.'

I was obliged to do this, inwardly praying that she would not wish to come. I had no need to be concerned.

'I've never cared much about the villagers,' she said coldly. 'I'm too old to start bothering now. If you have this whim to help people, you will find plenty in Witton in need of help.'

It was my first victory. Within a few weeks I was on friendly terms with Mrs Everett, the vicar's wife, and the people of Witton soon came to know me. Gradually my first, raw grief for my father began to fade. I took a genuine pleasure in seeing sad faces brighten when I walked over the doorstep of some cottage; the children would look with eager eyes at my basket of dainties, carried by Nellie.

My husband appeared quite pleased with this state of affairs. He seemed to think I was beginning to settle down happily to being mistress of Battle Tower. And it was true that although I still had no allowance of my own, and little freedom, yet, somehow, things were better.

One afternoon I rode my chestnut mare, Josty, down by the lake. It was early August. Soon the shooting season would begin, and I knew that both the men at Battle Tower were looking forward to it.

To my surprise, Herbert Webber appeared, also on horseback. He removed his hat, very ostentatiously, revealing his thin, lank strands of reddish-brown hair.

'Does Basil know you're riding alone in the grounds?' he asked, in what was intended to be a roguish tone of voice.

'He knows I exercise Josty,' I answered distantly.

'He's very jealous — although I expect you've found that out by now.'

I made no reply.

'He'd probably be jealous if he saw us here together.'

'Would he?' I could not keep the contempt out of my voice. I did not care for my husband, but I thought his cousin little short of detestable.

'He wasn't jealous over the first Mrs Webber, of course. He liked her veiled, and preferably in her room. Yes, she was terrible to look at, all right. But she served her purpose. *She* was no penniless bride. Mother and I had no quarrel with her.' He gave his unpleasant snigger. 'You're rather different, Maura.'

'Do excuse me. I must be getting back to the house. I usually take tea with my husband,' I said coldly. I turned Josty's head round.

'I'll come back with you. I advise you not to be so high-handed towards me. It would pay you, in fact, to be friendly. We might be able to help each other — we might even be able to do — well, what shall I call it? Business with each other.'

'I cannot think of any business I could possible have with you.'

'Can't you?'

He gave his unpleasant laugh again. The next moment he brought his horse right alongside Josty, and lunged forward, seizing me in a tight embrace, half dragging me out of the saddle.

I was taken completely by surprise. Shudders of dislike ran through me as his loose, sensuous mouth pressed on mine. His grip was so strong that I was quite unable to move, until, suddenly, he released me.

'How dare you?' I cried, almost choking with rage and disgust. 'How dare you behave thus with your own cousin's wife? What would you say if I told my husband — '

He gripped my arm with unpleasant hardness. 'You won't say one word to your husband, my dear. Not one little word. I could tell him a different story altogether. You might find yourself with as little freedom as the first Mrs Webber. But for a different reason, though.'

'Don't you have any loyalty towards him?' I burst out.

'Loyalty?' He laughed. Then his eyes narrowed to slits in his long, pale face.

'I hate him! But I conceal it very well — which is more than can be said for you sometimes — you don't exactly like him yourself, do you? But he has one great virtue — money. With money, the most unlovable people are tolerated, because they can buy anything. They can even buy a wife, as they would buy a thoroughbred horse, and for the same purpose! He's hateful, isn't he?'

For a moment I was silent, faced with the truth. I could not deny that I disliked my husband, but I would not admit it to this man. I felt afraid. Herbert Webber would, if he could, force me into a position where he could take liberties with me, and I should not dare say anything to my husband. I was just beginning to gain a little freedom for myself; I was fearful of losing it. He laughed again.

'Yes, think it over, my dear. And now you had better be off to present your dutiful self to your husband. I'll ride just behind you, so I can have a good view of you in the saddle.'

Afterwards, in the house, as Nellie helped me off with my riding habit, I wondered how any girl could possibly get into a situation as unpleasant and complicated as I had. I was living a lie; trying somehow to make a life with a husband I did not love.

On top of that, I now realized I would have to be very careful as far as Herbert Webber was concerned. That brief conversation had revealed something else to me — the younger man's loathing of his cousin. Not only his loathing, but his grasping, greedy spirit. He envied Basil Webber with a burning, intense envy; envied him his money, his power — yes, and envied him his wife. A shudder ran through me.

To survive as a human being at Battle Tower, I would have to be as cunning as everyone else.

Basil and I had tea together in the blue drawing room. I greeted him cheerfully, and he rose and kissed me with alacrity. I had schooled myself carefully to hide my distaste on such occasions. He appeared to be in a good mood.

'Well, Maura, the shooting season is about to begin, and we must send out some invitations for a shooting party.'

I poured the tea, and put his sugar in for him, as he liked me to. Two lumps. He stirred it slowly.

'That will be very pleasant,' I said.

'We will have all the best shots in the county here. We will invite the Ancrofts, of course. I hear the younger brother is at home, and recovering very well.

Probably he will be pleased to come.'

He reached out and squeezed my hand. His touch was as clammy and hateful as ever. I smiled serenely, and remarked that I was looking forward to it. Inwardly, though, my feelings were very mixed. I would see Charles again, not as a schoolgirl this time, but as the second Mrs Webber. What was he going to think? Did it matter, anyway? I was imprisoned, in the prison of marriage.

At dinner that evening, Mrs Webber remarked that she was tired, and thought she had a cold coming on. Basil told her absently to take care. Her son said nothing; merely sneaked a glance at me between courses.

'If I don't feel better for this shooting party — ' she left the sentence unfinished, and hitched her shawl more closely around her.

'If you don't feel better, then you may stay in your room,' remarked my husband. 'Your presence is not a necessity, delightful though it is. Maura is the hostess here now.'

'Of course, Basil,' she agreed hurriedly, looking at me with dislike.

The following day she took to her room, and we prepared for the shooting party. The weather was dry and sunny, although the wind was keen. When the first guests began to arrive at Battle Tower, in spite of everything, I felt a glow of pleasure. Both the Ancroft brothers came. I was tensed up as I received them. Charles was paler and thinner than I remembered him. He bowed very formally. The stricken look in his eyes when he raised them to mine made it very difficult for me to keep up an outward show of serenity.

'Mrs Webber — at your service.'

For a moment I was too overcome to say anything. Fortunately he turned to my husband.

'I must congratulate you, sir, on your great good fortune. And I hope you will be very happy, Mrs Webber.'

Something in his voice moved me unbearably. The charade I was acting out seemed hollow and useless. Happy!

I could never, never, be that as Basil Webber's wife. But we were about to dine, and I composed myself.

My husband led the way into the dining room with a large and imposing matron; I came last of all with Michael Ancroft, who, despite his mode of living was still considered the most important man among the guests. Charles was just in front of us; I had known beforehand that, willy-nilly, I would be seated between the two Ancroft brothers.

As we sat down, I caught the look of pride in my husband's eyes as he glanced at me. I was dressed in mauve lace, with tiny black bows as trimmings, and wearing diamond earrings which were carefully locked away by Gregory, the valet, when they were not in use.

The table looked magnificent, with the gleaming silver candelabra, and the floral arrangement which I had done, and which would have gladdened Mrs Chorley's heart. I suddenly thought of that veiled, tragic woman, whose wealth had been so useful to my husband.

What promises he must have made to her, what lies he must have told her, to gain her for his wife. An involuntary shiver ran through me.

'Are you cold, Mrs Webber?' came Charles' voice. Strange, he had asked me that once before, when my father and Amelia had gone off on honeymoon.

'No — not really,' I replied in some confusion. 'I was sorry to hear you were taken ill in Gibraltar, and I trust you are improving now.'

'I am regaining my health rapidly.'

There was a silence between us. Michael talked to a stout lady on his right, and the soup was served. Charles crumbled a roll nervously before he spoke again. 'This marriage is — well — a surprise.'

Our eyes met then, and what I saw in his disturbed me in a way I had not thought possible. Puzzled and unhappy they looked at me as though wanting me to deny it. If only I could!

'We were married in the spring,' I said.

'I did not think when I last saw you . . . ' His voice died away

'No,' I said softly. 'We cannot always see ahead.'

'You were still at school. I wanted to write to you, but I knew it would not be permitted — '

'Please,' I said, in a low voice. 'Do not talk in that manner. It is too late now.'

Too late! Glancing round the room, the splendour of everything seemed to mock me. The butler, the liveried footmen moving silently about, the great chandelier overhead, the company assembled round the table, the very jewels which decorated me; how tawdry and worthless they seemed.

'I was so sorry to hear about your father,' Charles began again.

'The shooting accident happened in the winter. I married in the spring, so my life has changed completely since you last saw me.'

'It must have been a sorrowing year for you.'

172

'It has been,' I said simply. I did not qualify that statement.

We then talked about other things. I wanted above all to avoid discussing my marriage, or any of the circumstances which had led up to it. I saw the unspoken question in Charles' eyes when they met mine. He knew well enough that this was no marriage of love, not on my side, anyway. Later in the evening, we gathered in the drawing room. Mrs Webber was keeping to her room, but as usual, her son appeared to be enjoying himself.

I moved among my guests as befitted a hostess, and yet I was only truly aware of the presence of one person, and that was Charles. And I knew that he felt the same way about me. It was as though some spell had been laid on us.

That night I lay, wakeful in bed, beside the sleeping form of my husband. I had thought that somehow I would be able to make my marriage bearable. But I had not reckoned with Charles coming back into my life — I had not reckoned with this tumult of feeling which I was experiencing. The look in Charles' eyes when he had first greeted me as Basil Webber's wife — I could not forget it.

I lay there in the darkness, wanting to turn over, but afraid of waking my husband. Charles had wanted to write to me at school, but knew that it would not have been permitted. I lay thinking about him. And a great fear rose in me, because I knew I could have feelings for him which I could never have for my husband. I tried to put the thought to one side, but without success. I knew that I must avoid being alone with Charles Ancroft at all costs. But above all else, that was what I wanted to be. Alone with him.

12

The shooting party was a success. I went out of my way to make everyone enjoy it. I caught Charles looking at me on several occasions, and knew that he wanted to be alone with me, too. It was impossible, or so I thought, but somehow on a sunlit, golden day, we found ourselves together. Charles had dropped behind; some of the ladies in the party had decided to go back to the house, and I said I would follow them.

'I've decided I've had enough for one day. If you are returning to the house, I will accompany you.' Charles' voice was serious; so were his eyes. I knew then that this was inevitable. I had feared being alone with him, but longed to be at the same time. Without speaking I fell into step beside him, and we walked in silence for a few moments.

'We can go this way — through the

copse and down by The Wilderness,' he said. For a moment I hesitated. The dark, August trees stood in front of us in their full beauty. It was sheltered and silent in the copse. A slow trembling seemed to be welling up inside me.

'Very well,' I said. There seemed to be no one about. As soon as we were screened by the trees, Charles slipped his hand in mine.

I knew that it was wrong; that it was dangerous and foolish, but I did not care.

He drew me under the shelter of an oak tree.

'Maura, why did you marry him? Why?'

'I had to,' I said dully. 'Papa had nothing — only debts. I had nothing — what else could I do? Mr Webber got a specialist for Papa — he paid his debts, and saved his good name. He said that if I married him, I could always keep Nellie; he said it was just a matter of a new home for Nellie and me — '

I broke off, remembering with bitterness how he had lied to me. Charles put his arms round me, and held me close.

'If only you had waited — just a little time — ' he whispered.

'How could I? Papa was gravely ill, and worried about money. Don't you understand, I was forced into this marriage?'

I burst into tears. I knew that I should not behave like this; that my defences were down, and that Charles knew what a mockery this marriage was. For a moment he stood holding me without speaking. I blinked away the tears, and looked into his face. His lips pressed down on mine. I knew that it was wrong and foolhardy; that it was sinful and wicked, and everything else. But something stronger than all that urged me on to return his kisses. It was like a storm breaking loose inside me; it was like being starved, and feasting.

This was what love was; what loving a man should be. I felt at that moment that all I wanted was to be locked in his arms for ever. Nothing else mattered; nothing at all.

He released me, and I swayed slightly, breathless.

'We mustn't do that,' I said, in a muffled voice. 'It's no use, Charles.'

'I love you, Maura.' The despair in his voice went through me like a physical pain. How could life be so cruel, so unjust? If he had not come back like this, perhaps I could have borne being married to Basil Webber.

'Tell me you love me too. Tell me.'

'You must not ask me to say things like that — must not — ' The next moment I was swept into another embrace. The hot, sweet passion of those kisses ran through me like a flame. My whole body was alive, and thrilling to his touch. For a few minutes only Charles' kisses were real, and my married life seemed like a dream. But how wrong, how terribly wrong were these feelings!

'We had better make for the house,'

he said huskily, a few minutes later. This was only commonsense. I could not neglect my guests, nor would it do for me to be seen alone in the company of Charles. I felt like a wrongdoer, and yet, foolhardy though I knew it was, I wanted his kisses on my lips.

After that first, wonderful experience of realizing that I loved him; of knowing what love could be like, I knew that happiness for me could never exist without him.

It was frightening, wonderful, and beautiful all at once. As Nellie was helping me dress for dinner that evening, she remarked how well I was looking. I was wearing a wine coloured gown, plain at the front, falling in tiers at the back. She arranged it carefully over my bustle. Looking in the mirror I could see that my eyes were bright, and my cheeks flushed.

'Oh Nellie,' I said, 'I've had such a happy afternoon.'

'Well, Miss Maura, I'm pleased to hear that. There's been little enough

179

happiness for you for long enough.'

'No, I'm not really happy,' I said. 'It's more like thinking you were dead, and being alive after all.'

And that was how I felt. As though something crushed deep inside me had risen again, and was singing aloud. And yet, on the other hand was the feeling of hopelessness. And fear. Fear of my own emotions, and fear of anybody discovering my secret. True, I was handling my husband better now; he was much more co-operative. But Herbert Webber . . . cold shivers ran down my spine at the thought of him. All he wanted was the chance to gain some sort of power over me. Nellie fastened a string of pearls round my neck.

'You look beautiful, Miss Maura. But take care.'

'I will, Nellie. Have no fear,' I said.

For Nellie knew as well as I did that she could be banished from the house at Basil Webber's whim. I went down into the drawing room. Mrs Webber had decided she was better, and was busy discussing her health with anyone who would listen.

That evening I was the perfect hostess; when my husband looked at me it was with great pride, he obviously thought I was doing him credit. But even though I paid no more attention to Charles than to any of the other gentlemen, I was aware of his presence. There was a link between us; when our eyes met, his told me very plainly that he loved me. And I was filled with joy that it should be so, yet unhappy, too.

One or two of the guests had brought their daughters with them. One of them, Berenice Muckle, a tall, thin fair girl, simpered wildly if Charles looked in her direction, and her mother was clearly very eager for him to look. After a day of fresh air and exercise, the evenings were spent fairly quietly. The ladies would retire to the drawing room, and leave the men in the dining room for a while.

Crochet work and embroidery would be brought out, and there would be a certain amount of gossip. I was pretty sure that my marriage to Basil Webber was the subject of a good deal of talk, although not of course at a house party at Battle Tower.

'Lieutenant Ancroft is recovering very well,' remarked Mrs Muckle. 'What a fine young man he is, to be sure.'

'And a splendid shot,' said Berenice, eagerly. 'He told me how much he was enjoying being here, Mrs Webber.'

'I hope everyone is enjoying it,' I said smoothly.

But something in Berenice's attitude roused despairing feelings inside me. Charles was, after all, a single man. Even though the Ancrofts were in much reduced circumstances, they were still the Ancrofts. The Muckles were wealthy, and Berenice was the only child . . .

The gentlemen joined us at this point, and the talk became more general. My husband offered to play the piano for anyone who cared to sing, and after much giggling and being coaxed by her mother, Miss Muckle sang 'My Love Is

Like A Red, Red Rose'. She had an incredibly high, thin, voice, with a pronounced trill in it. Everyone applauded warmly when she had finished, particularly her red-faced, loud-voiced father, and her eager mother.

Charles' eyes met mine across the room, and I caught a glint of amusement in them. I knew then that I need not trouble myself about Miss Muckle. It was a source of comfort to me in a way.

And yet, the torment of being in the same room as him; of knowing that although we loved each other, we must remain mere acquaintances in the eyes of the rest of the company . . .

We finished the house party with a ball. Since our brief sojourn in the copse, Charles and I had not been alone together. A whispered word or two; once, very daringly, he had managed to squeeze my hand in a crowded room.

When Nellie had finished arranging my hair, and dressing me for the ball, my husband appeared without warning.

I was sitting at the dressing-table. He came up behind me, and stroked my bare neck and shoulders.

'You are blossoming, Maura,' he said, and there was a note of smug satisfaction in his voice. 'You are becoming everything I could desire in a wife.'

A cold supper was being served that evening, instead of a formal dinner. The musicians began to play, and my engagement card was soon full. Charles booked two dances.

'When shall we meet again?' he whispered, as we waltzed together. 'Do you ever ride in the grounds alone?'

'Frequently,' I said. 'My husband usually plays golf in the afternoons. Sometimes I go into Witton to visit the sick, or else exercise my horse in the grounds.'

My heart was thudding with fear and excitement.

'We could meet at the old cottage, then. I know every inch of the grounds.

I'll ride over from The Little Manor House. I know where to tether my horse, and I can come the rest of the way on foot.'

'But ... I dare not meet you, Charles!'

'Dare not? I must see you, Maura! I must talk to you.'

Fear and longing fought inside me. But I could not deny my love. I had not the strength to say I would not meet him. Even as we made our arrangements, I thought of Herbert Webber. I would have to be careful indeed.

When finally the house party broke up, my husband seemed well content with its success, and with me too. I was careful to help maintain this attitude.

With a rapidly beating heart, I went out on the appointed afternoon. Herbert Webber was confined to the house with a cold, so I had nothing to fear in that respect.

The derelict cottage was a forlorn looking place. The chimney was broken, and slates were missing off the roof.

Surprisingly enough, the small, thick panes of glass at the tiny windows were for the most part intact, although very dirty. I slipped Josty's reins over the forked branch of a young tree, and approached our trysting place. The door was slightly open, as usual, and as I reached it, it was pushed to one side. I gave an involuntary gasp, but Charles stood there, smiling.

'You came,' he said simply, and drew me inside the empty mustiness of that old cottage. For a long time we stood clasped in each other's arms, not speaking. It seemed so still and silent in there, after the keen wind outside. I had never actually been inside before. The floor was of stone, and a ladder led to an upstairs room. There was an open fireplace, and on the floor an axe, a hammer, and other oddments of a like nature.

'Not very comfortable, I'm afraid,' said Charles. 'Do you mind, Maura?'

'It's the only place where we can meet,' I said. 'And even then — oh,

Charles, I should not be here.'

'You should not be there,' he said bitterly, nodding in the direction of Battle Tower. 'Not as that man's wife, anyway.'

'I've told you,' I said. 'I could do nothing else at the time. And what can I do now, except please him? If I don't he has threatened to get rid of my nurse, Nellie. It is wrong — wicked of me to come here, I know.'

'It was wicked to make you go through a marriage like that.'

For some time we stood talking in this manner; going round in circles. Then we began kissing again, with the same frightening, passionate urgency as we had done in the copse. I had told Nellie that we were meeting that afternoon. Although she was happy for me, she was fearful too. But I knew that if the need arose, she would be ready to hasten out and warn me. Even so, I dare not stay long.

'My sick leave will not last much longer,' said Charles. 'We must meet whenever we can, up to then. And then we must try to work something out.'

'Work something out? What can we possibly work out? Oh, Charles, there is no future for us — for our love.'

I knew that Charles had only his army pay, and a very small allowance from his brother. It was little enough for a young man in his position. Apart from that, he could not bring any hint of scandal to the regiment; it was unthinkable. Nor could I do anything. I was penniless, with Nellie dependent on me. She was no longer young; it would be impossible for her to find another position.

My relationship with my husband was improving; he was beginning to indulge me. It would be dreadful if he found out I had met Charles in secret. Nellie would be banished instantly; what other punishment might follow I did not care to think about.

And yet, I wanted Charles with all my heart . . .

After about half an hour spent thus,

talking, kissing, holding each other close, we parted, with promises to meet again. It had been so much easier than I had imagined, and yet I was no less afraid of seeing him clandestinely. I saw him sooner than I expected, though. We dare not arrange to meet too often, but two days later I was driving into the village with Nellie in a dogcart, and recognized a man on horseback coming towards us. He was mounted on a grey hunter, and I could feel my cheeks flushing as soon as I realized who it was. As I ordered the coachman to draw up, Charles reined in his horse, and removed his hat.

'Good day to you, Mrs Webber.' He smiled, including Nellie in his glance. 'Are you on your way to the village?'

'Visiting the poor and sick,' I replied. 'Isn't it a fine day?'

'It is indeed. I hope we will soon be having the pleasure of your company at dinner. We will be sending out invitations shortly.'

So a visit to The Little Manor House

was imminent. I dare not tarry long talking, for I felt I could not trust any of the servants, other than Nellie. He seemed to read my thoughts, for he replaced his hat, saying he must not keep us from our good work.

With a farewell wave he cantered his horse away. I could not resist a backward glance.

'Oh, Nellie . . . ' I said under my breath. She squeezed my hand understandingly.

'I know how you must feel, Miss Maura. He is such a fine young gentleman — ah, if things could have been different.'

'I've been through all that with him,' I said miserably. 'They could not have been different.'

She gave a worried little frown. 'Do be careful, my lamb. You are playing with fire.' She shook her head, and yet I knew that she was prepared to aid and abet me in any way she could, so that I could meet Charles whenever possible.

When the invitation to dine at The

Little Manor House came, Mrs Webber said she did not feel very well, and thought she would decline to go.

'I think you should have the doctor,' said her son. He turned towards me. 'I presume you are well, Maura?'

'Thank you — quite well.'

We were in the sitting room which we usually used when the four of us were together. My husband was in the library, looking for a book which had been mislaid. Herbert Webber had not removed his black velvet smoking jacket, and the scent of cigars still hung heavily around him.

'You look tired, Mother,' he went on, a solicitous note in his voice. 'Perhaps if you retired early, you might feel better.'

Mrs Webber put down the embroidery she had been languidly doing.

'I think perhaps you may be right, Herbert. In fact, I will go to bed now.'

She rose, and Herbert opened the door for her. 'Ask the maid to bring you a nightcap — it will help you sleep. Goodnight, Mother.' I stood up too, feeling vaguely apprehensive, however, there was nothing I could do, save bid her goodnight. I was alone with Herbert Webber. No sooner had the door closed behind his mother, than he seized me in a tight embrace.

'Stop it! How dare you?' I gasped.

'Quite easily.'

'I'll — I'll tell Basil.'

'I'll tell Basil, too! I'll tell him of the sly glances that pass between you and Ancroft — he was too busy playing host to see what I saw. You even managed to have a little walk through the copse together one day, did you not?' He grinned tauntingly at me.

'It has nothing to do with you,' I said coldly. 'As the hostess here, I can accompany a house guest walking in the grounds without arousing comment.'

'Most certainly. And what matter if it takes you a long time to walk through the copse? Don't put on airs and graces with me, dear cousin. Or I might be tempted to make things awkward for you.'

He pulled me towards him again, and I was too afraid to protest. His wet, brandy-smelling mouth was pressed down on mine; his hateful hands caressed my bare neck and shoulders, while I stood shuddering with distaste.

I wondered how much more pretending I would have to do; how much more I would have to endure in that house. There were footsteps in the corridor outside, and he released me immediately.

'Sit down,' he muttered, and made a pretence of attending to the fire, for which it was usual to ring for a maid. I sat down hastily, and took up my embroidery, just as the door opened. My husband entered the room, and for once, perhaps, I was not sorry to see him. I was still breathing quickly, but I bent over the drawn thread work which I was doing.

Basil looked slightly surprised to see us together.

'Where is your mother?' he enquired of his cousin.

'She has retired. She does not feel too well,' explained Herbert. He put down the fire-tongs, and wiped his hands with his handkerchief. 'She says she will not be dining at The Little Manor House this week.'

'Indeed? Then the three of us will go.'

He sat down and began to leaf through the pages of the book which he had been searching for. I still felt tense; it was a relief when I heard a scratching at the door, and got up to let in my husband's retriever, Mustard. I could not but like him; he was a fine dog, and knew me well by now. Indeed, I found him infinitely preferable to the Webber family.

'Perhaps someone would care to play chess,' suggested my husband. To my relief, Herbert said he would, and in the near-silence that followed while the two men played, I was able to regain my composure.

Later that week I went out on Josty to see Charles again. I was thankful that my husband was so interested in golf.

He still played most afternoons, new wife or not. Sometimes Herbert Webber joined him, when he was not attending to some business on the estate. His mother seemed to spend most of her afternoons lying down.

At the cottage, I dismounted, and tethered Josty. Hearing my footsteps, Charles appeared at the door.

'Darling!'

With wildly beating heart, I entered the cottage, and was clasped in his embrace. My feelings were so intense that for the next few minutes I felt I didn't care about anything; even the fear of being discovered left me.

'I wish there was somewhere for us to sit,' said Charles, looking round the room. 'Never mind, this is the best we can do, I'm afraid. I'm so thankful you managed to come.'

'So am I,' I whispered. 'Being with you makes me forget everything. But I'm so afraid, darling. I'm afraid of Herbert Webber.'

'Herbert Webber? Why?'

Rather hesitantly I told him of Herbert Webber's attitude towards me, and my unpleasant experience when left alone with him. Charles was enraged.

'How dare he! The disgusting, contemptible — '

He broke off, as though suddenly aware of his helplessness in the face of this situation.

'Oh, God, Maura, what can we do? It's an intolerable situation — intolerable. I can't bear the idea of not seeing you, but I'm afraid. The only thing we can do is be as careful as possible. Try to ensure that you are never alone with him for a moment. But we can't go on like this, darling. There must be some way out.'

Locked in his arms it almost seemed possible that there was a way out, and yet I knew well enough that there was not. That cottage, damp and unpleasant though it was, smelling of mustiness, was nevertheless a sort of haven. For a while we didn't speak at all, only enjoyed the sense of closeness and tenderness which we both felt. Even so, my tears were not very far from the surface. We parted with many tender assurances that we would meet there again. But before then I would be dining at The Little Manor House.

'Michael Ancroft seems to be making a bit of an effort socially on his brother's behalf,' remarked my husband later in the week, when we were getting ready to go to their house. 'Just as well young Charles went into the army; not that it's a bad idea for a second son anyway, even if he has money — not that the Ancrofts have any now. But I would be well content if my second son chose the army.'

Nellie had been dismissed, and we were alone in my room. I felt myself growing tense at his words. He bent and kissed the nape of my neck. 'You are young and healthy, Maura. The sooner you have a child, the better pleased I shall be. And the better for you, too.'

I forced myself to smile, whatever my feelings.

'Come, we must not be late,' said my husband.

The wind was cool as we drove along the narrow lanes to The Little Manor House. Basil and I sat together, while Herbert lounged in the seat opposite, the usual irritating little smirk hovering around his mouth. I wondered how Charles was even going to tolerate his presence after what I had told him.

Among the guests at the Ancrofts were quite a number of people who had attended our shooting party, including the Muckle family. Charles looked splendid in the dress uniform of the Northumberland Fusiliers. My feelings were almost unbearable as I sat there at the same table as the man I loved, with my husband there too, and Herbert Webber, his beady eyes gleaming, sitting opposite me. Where was it all going to end?

'You will be rejoining your unit shortly, I understand,' boomed Mr Muckle to Charles.

'In a few weeks, sir. I am pretty well

recovered now, anyway.'

'Glad to hear it. We're giving a ball for Berenice shortly. Mostly her hunting friends, you know. Naturally, all guests at this table will be welcome. We'll be sending out official invitations next week.'

Berenice simpered, and her mother smiled encouragingly at Charles. My husband glanced across at me, and I lowered my eyes, lest I should betray my feelings with an unguarded look. Later, we all assembled in the drawing room, and once again Berenice's quavering voice was raised in song.

I dare not look at Charles while she was singing, as I had a strong feeling that despite all our troubles, if I did he would be bound to burst out laughing.

Going home in our carriage at a late hour, both my husband and Herbert seemed in a jovial mood. I knew they had both been drinking quite freely.

'It's plain to see what the Muckles are hoping for,' said Herbert, with a grin.

'Quite plain,' agreed my husband.

'And a very good idea too. When it is necessary for a man to marry money, then he must do so, whatever the disadvantages in other ways. On the other hand, when a man can afford to pick and choose, then he will look for different qualities.'

'Certainly. A combination of beauty and good breeding are highly desirable qualities, too, in a wife — for a man of wealth,' agreed Herbert, glancing in my direction. 'In such a case, it is not important for the wife to have money. Indeed, with all her other assets, it could be a positive advantage for her *not* to have money. She is well aware then that she can do nothing and be nothing without her husband, and she is content to please him in all things.'

'You are quite right in your observations, Herbert.'

'Certainly *you* have chosen wisely,' went on Herbert. 'Maura is a credit to you, possessing as she does all the qualities one hopes for in a wife, as well as beauty.'

I was detesting the turn the conversation had taken, and well Herbert Webber knew it. He was enjoying baiting me like this.

'Undoubtedly young Ancroft will marry the ugly, squeaky-voiced Miss Muckle. Don't you agree, Maura?'

'I had not thought about it,' I said coldly, repressing a yawn.

'Are you tired?' enquired my husband.

'A little.'

I knew, though, that feigning tiredness would not prevent him coming to my room, particularly after he had been drinking. Nor did it, indeed. The compliments which I had received during the evening, and the conversation in the carriage with Herbert seemed to have inflamed his desire to fever pitch. Added to that was his determination to beget an heir.

When at last he slept, I lay, miserably wakeful, knowing that I could not endure this life with him. I knew well enough that my present problems had come about purely as a result of marrying Basil Webber.

And yet, under pressure from him and from circumstances, what else could a girl of my age have done? I was trapped; doomed.

13

I sobbed this out to Charles when I next saw him, at the cottage. He gathered me close in his arms, and covered my wet cheeks with his kisses.

'There *must* be some way out,' he said. 'We belong together, Maura — we have done right from the start. The best thing I can think of is that when I have to go away, we write to each other, and think what there is to be done about the situation.

'How can we write?' I said despairingly.

'Surely I could write to your maid, Nellie? Maura, my darling, I cannot ask you to run away with me and live with me! I cannot ask you to face scandal and hardship — and being poor, for my sake. Don't you see, I simply cannot ask it of you.'

'I love you,' I said obstinately.

Then I thought how it would affect Charles if we ran off together. He would be obliged to resign his commission in the Northumberland Fusiliers. The scandal would be dreadful. Almost as if he were reading my thoughts, Charles said: 'And my brother would suffer. Your husband would put certain business pressures on him which he withholds now. Things are more complicated than you think, Maura.'

I nestled in his arms, an apathy of hopelessness creeping over me. 'There is nothing, then,' I said. 'Only despair.'

'And a few hours of snatched happiness.'

He began to shower kisses on my face and lips. Our passion, always close to the surface, suddenly rose up with a force that frightened me, and swept us both into another world.

Charles put his cloak down on the hard dustiness of the floor, and we lay together. We did not stop to think, to reason, or to do anything of that nature. The wild feelings which ran unchecked through my body made me realize only too well the difference between my odious marriage, and what a union with one I loved would be like.

Afterwards we lay clasped in each other's arms, shaken as though by a tremendous storm.

'I must go, Charles,' I whispered at last. The tenderness between us seemed almost unbearable, it was so intense. Even so, I was overwhelmed with guilt, and told him so.

'Would you feel better if we became man and wife in the sight of God? Clasp my hand, and say that you take me to be your husband in the sight of God.'

We clasped hands in that squalid little cottage, and exchanged our simple vows. In my heart I felt that we were truly married because of what we felt for each other. But I knew that to the outside world we were still sinners, and only my marriage to Basil Webber counted.

With a last embrace we parted, and

planned to meet later in the week. I urged Josty along at a gallop; coming out past The Wilderness I was surprised to see Herbert Webber ahead of me on horseback. At luncheon that day he had mentioned something about going into Witton to see the policeman about some poaching that was going on.

Why was he right in the opposite direction, then? Back at the house I took Josty into the stableyard, and hastened to my room, where Nellie removed my riding habit, which was more crumpled and dusty than it should have been.

What had taken place that afternoon was sacred and private between Charles and myself. I knew that I was still flushed and slightly dishevelled; she must have noticed, but she made no comment about it. Uneasily I told her that I had seen Herbert Webber in the grounds.

'I strolled about near the house — I saw no one,' said Nellie. 'Dear lamb, I hope all is well.'

She helped me with my toilet, brushed my hair, and hooked me into an expensive gown. I went to take tea with my husband.

The following morning I was arranging chrysanthemums in the dining room, when a footman appeared with an envelope on a silver salver. It was addressed to me, but unstamped. I walked over to the window and opened it. It was just a few words on plain notepaper: 'My dearest Maura, please see me at the usual place today, early, at two o'clock. I cannot explain. It is very urgent. You must be there.' It was simply signed 'C'.

I went over to the brightly burning fire and dropped it in straight away. Then I stood, my heart beating wildly. What had happened? Why did he want to see me before we had arranged to? Who had delivered the letter to the footman? I could scarcely eat anything at luncheon.

It was a fine day, so I could count on Basil playing golf. He asked me how I intended to spend the afternoon.

'I'm going into Witton to see somebody who is ill,' I said glibly, feeling myself flush as I spoke. I kept my eyes down on my plate, and forced myself to eat.

'Well, very commendable of you, my dear,' said my husband. He spoke almost absently, his mind clearly on his golf.

Shortly after luncheon, I rode Josty along in the direction of The Wilderness. I had mentioned the note to Nellie, and she was as worried as I was, but she agreed that I would have to go if possible.

'Be careful, Miss Maura,' were her last words. There was no one about, and Josty went along at a gentle trot. When I came in sight of the cottage, it looked deserted as usual. I dismounted, tethered the horse and approached the house. As a rule, Charles met me at the door.

Uneasily I stepped over the threshold, and was immediately seized in a strong grip. A cry of terror broke from me as soon as I realized it was not my lover; it froze with horror when I looked into the leering face of Herbert Webber.

'So you came. Yes, you are on time, cousin. No, it is of no use to scream and struggle. Even if you had planned to meet your soldier-boy today, he won't be here yet — I know what time you meet. And whether he comes today or tomorrow, *you* will not be here. You will be in your room at Battle Tower, feeling indisposed.'

I was shaking with uncontrollable terror and shock. This hateful, evil man knew about Charles and me — he knew our meeting place! I felt physically sick as he held me with my arms pinioned down, an expression of gloating delight on his unpleasant face.

'Come — look pleased to see me. Kiss me, coz . . . you don't want to? Trying to pretend you don't do such things? Don't bother to pretend to me. I don't pretend to you. Basil's first wife died childless, and I was well pleased

— my mother too. She brought wealth, and no children. Then Basil takes up with an Irish chit like you; at his age he wants youth, beauty, and an heir. Well, I am the rightful heir to Battle Tower when the time comes — he had no business to marry you! My mother could act as mistress here — he could have women if he wanted them — a wife was not necessary. But no, he had to have you, and here you are, creeping out like some slut of a servant girl to meet your soldier-boy!'

'Let me go! How dare you say such things? I'll — I'll — '

'You'll what? Tell your husband? Tell him the outrageous things I've been saying in the old cottage where you sneak off to meet Charles Ancroft? You can do nothing except what I tell you — you dare not do otherwise.'

I felt too faint and sick to reply.

'Stupid and guileless as you are, you never questioned but that note came from Charles Ancroft, did you? And before we leave this hovel, there will be a note left for him. And don't say you won't write it; I have already written it. It is less trouble than making you. I'll read it to you if you like.'

With one arm linked firmly through mine, he produced a note from his pocket and read it.

'Dear Charles,' it ran. 'Please do not wait for me today or any other day, from now on. I have decided that I do not care for you, but that I love my husband, and my place is with him. Do not try to see me again, as I do not wish to see you. I just want to forget all about you; from now on I will make every effort to avoid you, and I want you to do the same with me.'

It was signed 'M'.

'Oh, please,' I gasped, 'you can't be as cruel as that! You can't leave a note like that! I love him — he loves me! You know that — it will break his heart, and mine too! Please — have pity on me! I've done you no harm — '

'Yes you have,' he said, smirking with enjoyment. 'I've told you, I didn't want

Basil marrying again, although I can well see why he wanted you. But he's not the only one who wants you, is he? It's my duty to protect my cousin's honour — to protect the name of Webber. We don't want alien blood in the family, do we?' His leering, tormenting face came closer to mine.

I tried to move my head away, but his mouth pressed down on mine. I felt faint with shock, disgust, and fear, all mingled together. He ran his hands over my body, and I squirmed with revulsion under my tight blue riding habit.

'Not . . . *alien* . . . blood,' he repeated slowly. 'You look like a little wild animal at bay, Maura — a little wild animal.' He laughed, and held me still tighter.

'Do you know the first thing you do when you tame gun dogs and other animals? You spit into their mouths; that's why girls are warned against being kissed. It tames them to the kisser.'

'Oh, God, if Charles came now — ' I

burst out, 'he would — '

'He would do nothing,' said my tormentor. 'Because there is nothing he could do. Your honour must be protected at all costs. Young Ancroft must, perforce, keep silent about this matter, just as you must.'

'Please let me write a note, then,' I begged. 'Please, Herbert, let me tell him in my own way. I'll give you anything — ' I pulled myself up sharply, but he had already seized on my words.

'What can you give me?' he asked tauntingly. 'You have nothing, my pretty coz — nothing but yourself! I'll take you up on that, though. You may write a note yourself, but on my conditions. It is not hard to guess what they are.'

No, it was not hard. He expected me to submit to his loathsome embraces first, an idea which filled me with disgust.

'Let go of me,' I said. 'Let me go back to the house.'

'So you are not prepared to comply with my conditions — for the time being, anyway. Later on, we will see . . . I have not finished with you yet, you little trollop! I could have you turned out of the house, if I chose.'

I longed to cry: 'Have me turned out, then!' but fear held me silent.

Fear of bringing disgrace and scandal on Charles; of ruining his career, and spoiling his life. Fear, too, that my husband would not turn me out, but would turn out Nellie, and make me suffer in other ways.

'You can come back to the house with me — and stay in your room for the rest of the day. Say you are not well, and didn't go into Witton. I shall be able to tell Basil that I've finally put a stop to the poaching that's been going on. I don't like poachers — unless *I* happen to be doing the poaching.'

I began to weep hopelessly. He threw the note on the floor, and pulled me outside with him.

'Shed no tears. Your husband would not be pleased if he saw you red-eyed; he might even want to know the source of your unhappiness, and that would never do. I am on foot, so you can walk back to the house with me, and lead your precious horse — you think a deal more of it than the man who gave you it, I know.'

We walked along, with me leading Josty by the reins. I could not put into words the misery and anguish I was feeling. The tears were rolling unchecked down my cheeks; I could not bear the thought of Charles coming to that cottage, and finding that brutal note.

Surely, surely, he would not believe it! Surely he would guess that I had been forced to write it. But whatever he thought, he might deem it best to keep away, for my sake. It was an unendurable situation — it was too cruel to be borne.

'I've told you — it's no use crying,' said my unwelcome escort impatiently. 'Control yourself, you can do that in private. Behind locked doors you can weep and swoon to your heart's content. And much good it will do you.'

The wind was rising; as we came out of the sheltering copse, it blew with force across the open land. I felt drained of strength.

'Let me get on Josty,' I said. 'I can't walk.'

Herbert Webber hesitated. 'You look a bit white. Very well, get on, but give me the reins.' Somewhat grudgingly he helped me mount, and we went along in silence. When finally we came in sight of the stables, my companion let go the reins, and watched me canter the horse into the stableyard. He waited for me, and we entered the house together.

'Now straight up to your room,' he said, in a low voice. 'And don't go near that cottage again. You will have cause for regret if you do.'

I picked up the skirt of my habit, and hurried to my room. I threw myself across the bed and sobbed, this time without tears. I lay there for a long time before I rang the bell for Nellie. When she saw me, there was no need for words.

'My lamb,' she said, 'my poor lamb — I told you to be careful.' With her usual resourcefulness she soon had me undressed and into bed, where she gave me a soothing draught, which she sent to the kitchen for. Having heard my sobbed-out story, she drew the curtains, and said she would tell the master I was indisposed, and had gone to bed.

'Should he come to see you, pretend you are asleep, Miss Maura.'

Much later in the day, I was not sure when, the door opened. I lay huddled under the bedclothes, scarcely daring to breathe. I knew that it was my husband, but he did not disturb me, neither then nor later. I slept alone that night, slept fitfully, in between periods of hopeless crying.

* * *

Under the circumstances, perhaps it was fortunate that I developed a chill. The following day I was running a temperature. Dr Parnaby was sent for, and said I must remain in bed for several days. Nellie seldom left the room during this period, except for when my husband came to see me. When I was up again, I looked frail and white, and the doctor forbade me to leave the house for a month, for which I was grateful. Invitations had to be refused, because I was indisposed. Rather to my surprise, even after a month I did not feel well.

One morning, giddiness and nausea overcame me when Nellie was lacing me. She led me back to the bed.

'You must know what is wrong with you, Miss Maura,' she said gently. 'You are going to have a child, and this, perhaps, will be the best thing that could happen. A baby will heal all this heartache.'

'How can it?' I asked despairingly. 'How can I go on living, Nellie, knowing that Charles would come to the cottage and read that note? How can I want this child, knowing that I can never love my husband? It is just a mockery — a cruel mockery.'

Mockery or not, Nellie was right. Dr Parnaby called in that morning, just to make sure that I had fully recovered. As I was still far from well, he examined me, and said he had some very good news for me and my husband; we could expect a child.

'Take things easy. The sickness will improve,' he said cheerfully.

He left the room, but had not been gone for more than a short while before my husband came, and dismissed Nellie from our presence. He came over to the bed. There was an air of excitement about him.

'The doctor has told me the news, Maura,' he said. 'At last I am to have an heir — a son of my own! This child will be the first of many, I hope. You must take the greatest of care of yourself. No riding, no hunting — just a gentle walk in the grounds from now on. Aren't you delighted?'

I forced myself to smile at him, as he so clearly expected it.

'Of course,' I said. 'But I don't want anyone else to know about this — not for some time, anyway.'

'I suppose that is quite natural,' said Basil. 'Delighted though I am about it, I understand your modest feelings, my dear. It will be known only to the two of us, and the doctor, for the time being — and your Nellie, I have no doubt.'

He smiled and walked over to the window, surveying the view. I had little doubt that he was thinking shortly there would be an heir to leave it all to. For the next two or three weeks I made the most of my indisposition: I kept to my room with my husband's approval, and spent long anguished hours thinking of Charles.

'Young Ancroft has rejoined his unit. I understand he is going abroad,' remarked Basil one day.

I caught my breath sharply. I dare not look at him, lest I betray my feelings.

'Nellie, I can't bear it,' I sobbed, later that day. 'I love him, and I will never see him again! Must I live the rest of my life with a man I cannot love? I was not to know what it would be like when he persuaded me to marry him. And now I must live with him and have his children; there is nothing but duty left, and I am only eighteen!'

As always, Nellie tried to comfort me. By now I was obliged to see the rest of the Webber family. Herbert said he hoped I was fully recovered. He spoke with a mocking smile on his face. His mother said she hoped there would be no more sickness in the house, adding that she herself never felt really well.

'I can't say I feel too well myself tonight,' remarked my husband. I noticed that he looked rather paler than usual, and that he was not eating. To my relief he had been sleeping in the dressing room ever since my chill; I do not know how I could have endured his embraces after that unforgettable, wonderful afternoon with Charles. At least I had nothing like that to fear while I was expecting this child. The next day he seemed really ill, and once again, Dr

Parnaby was sent for.

'It looks as though your husband is going to require some careful nursing,' he told me. 'It's not just a chill like you had, I'm afraid. This is just the beginning; all we can do is keep him in bed on a light diet. We will see what the next few days bring.'

14

They brought a steady worsening of my husband's condition.

Gregory, his valet, did a good deal of the nursing. Nellie and I nursed him too, and Herbert and his mother took it in turns to sit with him, and give him his medicine. It was so unexpected. I had thought his illness would only have lasted a few days, but Dr Parnaby told me it would be several weeks before he was completely out of danger. When I questioned him as to the nature of Basil's illness, he said vaguely that it was congestion of the lungs, 'with complications'. He added that there would be a good deal of strain involved in looking after him, and that I might have to engage the services of a nurse.

'It would never do for you to overtire yourself,' he said, adding that I had already had my share of sick-rooms that year. Basil was occupying a large guest room, with Gregory sleeping in the adjoining dressing room, as this seemed to be the most practical plan for the time being. As the patient appeared to be in pain, and could not sleep, the doctor prescribed a sleeping draught.

One desolate autumn afternoon, with the rain blowing in occasional gusts against the window, I settled down to sit with my husband. He was asleep, and the doctor instructed that he should have a sleeping draught if he woke in pain. The sick-room smelled of stale air. A great fire was roaring in the hearth, and even though the room was large, it was very warm. I picked up a book and began reading. After a while, I could no longer concentrate. I lay back in the armchair, and thought about Charles.

Although I was prepared to nurse my husband, and do all the things which I should do as a wife, there was no love; only duty.

Unbidden, the tears rose to my eyes.

While I was thinking these thoughts, I must have drifted off to sleep. A knock on the door woke me. To my surprise it was the parlourmaid, bearing a tray with my tea on. My husband was still asleep, and showed no signs of rousing. I ate my tea, and rang for the maid, giving her instructions that Gregory should take my place in the sick-room for a while. I felt I must have a turn in the grounds; just a breath of fresh air. Warmly dressed, and accompanied by Nellie, I walked on the terrace in front of the house. The wind was keen, and despite the constant sweeping up of the gardeners, the russet leaves blew about the place in great clouds, and settled in patches, clinging to our boots and skirts as we walked along.

At dinner that evening there was the usual discussion about the patient's condition.

'He's been asleep all afternoon. He was asleep when I left him with Gregory,' I said. 'I shall go to him again as soon as dinner is over.'

'He is fortunate indeed to have such a devoted wife,' said Herbert, with his hateful, mocking smile. I made sure I saw as little of him as possible. I had never been alone with him since that terrible afternoon when he had been waiting for me in the cottage. When I went to my husband's room later, he was still sleeping.

'Has Mr Webber roused at all?' I asked Gregory.

'Not at all, ma'am.'

Gregory looked tired. He was not a young man, and he had spent a good many hours at the bedside. His face was white with fatigue.

'You may go and have a rest, then. Take a few hours off. I'll stay with Mr Webber until it is time to prepare him for bed. Perhaps he will have a quiet night.'

'Very well, ma'am.' He left the room silently, and I took up my book again. The room was quiet, save for the sound of my husband's breathing, and the clock ticking on the mantelpiece. Later in the evening, I went over to the bed, and looked at the patient. How ill he looked, lying in that great fourposter bed, with its heavy blue brocade curtains.

How ill, and how old. He wore a moustache as a rule, but since he had been confined to bed his beard had been allowed to grow, too. It was a pepper-and-salt stubble, and his face was ashen. He showed no signs of waking at all. Gregory said that he had put fresh poultices on, and that the master had not roused while he had been doing it. Perhaps if he slept on, and through the night, it might mark the turning point in his illness.

I rang for Nellie to sit with me for the last hour, before Gregory took over night duty. She came in quietly.

'Mr Webber's been sleeping all day,' I remarked, when she appeared. She went over to the bed, and stood looking down at him by the light of the oil lamp, very much as I had done.

'He seems . . . peaceful,' she said at

last. She turned towards me. 'Are you all right, Miss Maura?'

'Yes,' I replied.

For a while we sat there in silence. I felt very heavy-hearted. Grieving for Charles; longing to feel his arms around me, yet I must sit in that stifling atmosphere with this sick man for whom I felt no love. What was Charles doing now? Disjointed thoughts ran through my mind. It seemed as though I was being punished for loving him. But surely he would never believe that cruel note left in the cottage.

★   ★   ★

The following morning, I visited Basil again. To my surprise, Herbert Webber was already there, talking in a low voice to Gregory.

'Good day, Maura,' said Herbert. 'We have already sent for the doctor. Basil seems to be breathing rather badly. Gregory came to tell me earlier, rather than disturb you unnecessarily.'

I looked at the figure in the bed. He was indeed breathing badly, with long, gasping sighs.

'Has he been poulticed lately?' I asked Gregory.

'An hour ago, ma'am. He has never woken.'

'Not at all?'

'Not at all.'

Herbert Webber shot a peculiar glance at me; sly, and yet, oddly excited. 'I stayed with him while Gregory had breakfast,' he said. 'I shall go for some coffee . . . you had better join me in the breakfast room, Maura.'

When Dr Parnaby arrived, Herbert brought him up to the sick-room, to which I had hastened after having a cup of coffee. Basil appeared much the same. Frowning slightly, the doctor examined him, sounding his chest very carefully.

'H'm,' he said thoughtfully, straightening up. He glanced at me. 'He's not so well,' he said slowly. 'I had thought there would be some improvement today . . . however, he is well propped up on the pillows. I'll call in later.'

He turned to Herbert. 'And of course, should there be any change in Mr Webber's condition — for the worse, I mean — send for me immediately.' He gave my shoulder an encouraging little pat.

'Try not to worry too much. People can seem very ill, and then they take a turn for the better. I've seen it many a time.'

But my husband did not take a turn for the better; in fact he never regained consciousness. Still sleeping, he slipped out of the world, thereby surprising a number of people. I had not loved him, far from it, but the shock of his death was unbelievable.

The next few days seemed a blur. There were letters to be written, and mourning to be ordered.

What I do remember, very clearly, is Nellie clasping both my hands in hers, and saying, in a voice hoarse with emotion: 'You're free, Miss Maura — you're free!'

The day of the funeral came and went, as such things do. Back in deepest mourning, I saw my husband buried. I had been a bride and a widow within a few months, now I was to be a mother.

As I stepped into the carriage to come home, I saw the silent, sympathetic faces of the villagers. Still numb with shock, I shrank back into the carriage seat.

'Well, *that's* over,' said Herbert Webber. 'And now for the will.'

I looked at him without speaking. His manner was almost jubilant. His mother produced a black-bordered handkerchief, and, raising her veil, dabbed her eyes.

'My poor cousin,' she said, to no one in particular.

'Yes, we all grieve,' said her son. 'We must give Basil's broken-hearted widow such comfort as we can.'

'I've no doubt you will deal very kindly with her, Herbert,' murmured his mother.

'Very kindly,' echoed Herbert smugly. Even though Nellie had reminded me that I was free, I could still not fully realize it. Sitting opposite Herbert Webber and his mother in the carriage, I began to wonder about other things. Undoubtedly my late husband must have left a will. I knew that both Herbert and his mother had resented Basil marrying me, for fear a child would come, and oust Herbert from his position as the 'rightful heir'.

As far as I knew, up to that last illness, Basil Webber had always enjoyed good health. But from his attitude, Herbert Webber knew that there was a will, and a will in his favour. Basil had never discussed things like that with me. What then would my position be now, and that of the child?

Back in the house we partook of madeira and biscuits, and then the reading of the will took place. One or two very distant relations of the deceased were there, looking suitably glum. Herbert sat with his mother, his usually pale face flushed with excitement.

Mr Redhead and his son Eric, who

had been my husband's solicitors, glanced round the room. Then Mr Redhead began to read the will. The first shock was when he read out the date, which was only three weeks before the death of my husband. I heard Herbert Webber draw in his breath sharply; the whole room seemed to gasp. I sat with my head bowed, as Mr Redhead read out my late husband's wishes. The heir to Battle Tower was to be the first-born son by his wife, Maura Elizabeth. In default of heirs male, it went to the eldest daughter. Should there be no issue at the time of his death, Battle Tower became mine; the entire estate.

Suddenly the whole room seemed to be in an uproar. Startled, Mr Redhead looked up over his spectacles.

'So now we know!' shouted Herbert Webber, his face pale again, but with fury. 'You put him up to that, you slut! You fooled my cousin, and then when he became ill, you saw your chance — '

'Please, sir!' Mr Redhead looked

nonplussed. 'I assure you, my client was very anxious to draw up a new will — '

'My son is the heir to Battle Tower,' declared Herbert's mother. There was no sign of the black-bordered handkerchief now. 'He's the rightful heir — the rightful heir!'

'It scarcely sounds so to me,' remarked one of the distant relations, a malicious smirk on his face.

'She's an imposter! She has no right to my inheritance,' went on Herbert. 'And anyway, I'm not satisfied with the way my cousin died. There are a number of things I'm not satisfied about.'

There was a momentary silence in the room, and then a loud buzz of chatter.

'Not satisfied?' boomed the distant relation, his face turning a mottled purple. 'What do you mean — not satisfied?'

'What I say! I put these thoughts to one side, but now — '

'I advise you to be very careful what

you say, sir,' said Mr Redhead, waving his spectacles at Herbert Webber.

'I wasn't asking for your advice,' was the tart reply.

'I am here, sir, for the purpose of reading my late client's will.'

'Yes!' shouted the purple-faced relative. 'Pray proceed with the matter.'

I sat there trembling. Herbert Webber shot me a baleful glance. My thoughts were in a turmoil as the solicitor proceeded with the reading of the will.

Although neither Herbert nor his mother had been left penniless, far from it, and although there were a number of bequests, I was mistress of Battle Tower. I thought of the child I was to bear; the secret known only to the doctor, myself, and Nellie. I had been very unhappy in my marriage; Basil Webber had married me because he wanted me, and because he wanted children by me.

He must have hurried to his solicitor as soon as he knew about the child, and drawn up a new will, ensuring straight away that Herbert was no longer the heir. And yet, he had ensured, too, that in the event of no issue, I would inherit Battle Tower.

How little he must have dreamed his death was so near, and how pleased he must have been about the child. So pleased that he had put me before his cousin.

Mr Redhead had finished now. Herbert glanced at me again, his mouth a thin, angry line.

Much later that day I lay on my bed, exhausted, with Nellie in attendance. I had told her of the will, and how I was now the mistress of Battle Tower. I still could not believe it, but Nellie threw her arms round me and wept.

'You can be happy, now, Miss Maura.'

'Happy?' I said. 'No, Nellie. Not that.'

'But things will be better. You see, after the child is born, everything will be different . . . '

* * *

The following day Herbert Webber sought me out, saying he had something of the utmost importance to discuss with me.

I agreed to see him alone in the library. Up to then I had not been in contact with him at all since his angry outburst during the reading of the will.

His manner had changed altogether now. He saw that I was comfortable, and that a good fire was burning in the hearth. He then coughed a trifle self-consciously, and after enquiring very solicitously about my health, he began to speak about Basil's death, and my circumstances.

'You do understand, Maura, that I was upset about things when the will was being read — that I did not really mean what I said?'

'Very well,' I said. 'I'll accept your word for it.'

'I thought you would understand. The thing is — you must have been aware for some time that I entertain certain feelings towards you. Oh, I know things have not been easy for you, married so young to a man like Basil. But caring for you as I did — as I do — I had to prevent you from meeting young Ancroft — from doing anything foolish, which you might have regretted. It may have seemed harsh at the time, but it was in your own interests, even though I know you hated me for doing it. But if you behave sensibly, as I'm sure you will, you can forget any past unhappiness. Think of the future — think of *our* future, Maura! We could have a wonderful life together — I would make you so happy!'

For a moment I stared at him in disbelieving horror. He was actually proposing — as if I had not had enough misery by marrying one Webber!

The coaxing expression on his face; the fixed smile; the ingratiating manner filled me with a disgust for him far greater than any I had felt before. This despicable, loathsome creature was proposing marriage to me as a means of gaining Battle Tower! Since the reading of the will, he had thought things over, and decided this was his best plan.

'I know you would soon grow to care for me,' he went on, his eyes eager.

'Please don't waste your time, or mine either,' I said coldly. 'Your motives are very obvious. While my husband was alive, I was bound to tolerate your presence in this house — and that of your mother. I am mistress of Battle Tower, the will made that very plain. You will do me a great favour by removing yourself and your mother away from this house as speedily as you can. And I have nothing further to say to you — nothing. Accept the fact that I have no esteem for you at all — none. And now I shall go to my room and rest.'

Instantly, Herbert Webber's face changed. He flushed up, and his eyes grew malevolent. As I rose, he caught my arm angrily.

'If you won't see sense, then I'll have a bit of investigating done. It's true that I'm not satisfised with certain things connected with Basil's death, and I warn you, I shan't hesitate to go to the utmost lengths — the utmost lengths — if you persist in your high-handed attitude towards me! I'm giving you a choice — I shall have a postmortem on Basil — or you agree to my proposal. Which is it to be?'

'Stop attempting to frighten me,' I said, trying to shake his grip off my arm. 'I really don't know what you're talking about, but one thing I do know. You are repulsive to me; your very presence in this house insults me, and I find the idea of marriage to you quite unspeakable.'

I wrenched myself away with a quick movement, and hurried to the door. Herbert Webber made no attempt to detain me. His cold eyes were blazing with venom.

'You wait,' he said, his voice hoarse with restrained fury. 'You're going to regret those words. You're going to beg for mercy before I've finished. I'm convinced that Basil died from an overdose of that sleeping draught. I overheard Gregory telling the house-keeper how the bottle had gone down between luncheon and evening, the day before he woke me early to get the doctor. Oh, yes, my girl, I'm going to get the police in on this.'

I left the room, my heart thudding with fear, in spite of keeping outwardly calm. What did he mean? The day before the doctor was brought in early was the day I had fallen asleep in the sick-room.

'Nellie, Herbert Webber has threat-ened to have Basil's body exhumed — he says he wants an inquiry into his death! As if I haven't had enough to bear,' I told her.

Her face turned a chalky white. 'What can he be thinking of? What — '

'He never mentioned any suspicions about this before,' I said. 'And who on earth would want to — want to — '

Like Nellie, I was stricken into silence.

* * *

241

After all that had gone before, having my husband's body exhumed seemed the last straw. The Webbers knew nothing of the expected child, nor had I any intention of telling them.

And if Herbert Webber had suspected foul play, he had kept very quiet until the will was read. But, doubtless, he had thought to inherit Battle Tower.

As Basil enjoyed good health, and we had only been married a few months, there was no reason why he should rush to change his will. And, in fact, he had not rushed, not until he knew of the coming child. If he had not known so quickly, undoubtedly he would have died with the will unchanged, and Herbert Webber named as the rightful heir. Now he set the wheels of the law in motion, and life became a nightmare; a nightmare of questions, of trying to remember things; trying to keep some vestige of self-control.

Although Dr Parnaby had been rather surprised at the way Basil had died, he had not questioned his death in any way. But the tests and examinations which were made revealed that Herbert Webber was right in his suspicions. Allegations, accusations; these things followed. People talking; police at the house; the whole, ponderous weight of the law suddenly, terrifyingly, directed at me. And then, one bitterly cold day, they took me away to await the Assizes. I remember the icy numbness that crept over me, the disbelief; the terror on Nellie's face. I was charged with the murder of my husband.

Later, at the trial, every hour of that day when I fell asleep in the room was carefully gone through. I was questioned again and again about little things which I had scarcely noticed.

I had not taken particular notice of the bottle of sleeping draught on the table near my husband's bed. Gregory, giving evidence, said that the bottle had been quite full, and that when he had come into the room to relieve me while I went out for some fresh air, he noticed it was considerably less.

He admitted that he himself had left

the room for about twenty minutes to take tea with the housekeeper, because his master was so soundly asleep.

He had, however, told the housekeeper about the amount which had gone from the bottle, and this was overheard by Herbert Webber. By the merest chance he had been in the stables, and had accidentally cut his finger. It was only a superficial cut, but as it was bleeding quite profusely, he thought it best to go into the house the back way, and ask the housekeeper for something to put on it. It was then that he overheard Gregory talking.

Now, of course, the fact that I was to have a child became known . . . if only Basil had not made a new will only three weeks before his death! And yet, I had known nothing of it — nothing. But the case against me seemed to grow ever stronger. How cunning Herbert Webber was. He did not mention Charles, as I thought he might.

As he was the only one apart from Nellie who knew of those few meetings in the cottage, he probably thought that it would merely be his word against mine; as he could prove nothing, he kept silent. Moreover, although Charles was abroad, Michael was not; Herbert Webber was a coward as well as a bully; with Michael Ancroft to reckon with, he dare not drag Charles' name into the trial.

His evidence was backed by his strong inference that I had married Basil purely for his money. How could I explain the peculiar position I had been put in; how could I talk about my father's debts? In any case, to marry for money is one thing, to commit murder is quite another.

Trembling and sick, at last I took my place in the witness box, where I was allowed to sit down after taking the oath.

The whole thing seemed unreal to me; the bewigged, florid-faced judge with his merciless stare; my faltering voice answering the questions; the sea of curious faces watching from the public gallery. I had been told that if the verdict went against me, they would not hang me until after the child was born.

Endless, endless questions . . .

'Now, Mrs Webber, think very carefully about that afternoon. At what time did you enter your husband's room?'

I heard my voice replying slowly, as from a long way off:

'I believe it was between half past one, and two o'clock.'

'And you did not notice how much sleeping draught there was in the bottle beside his bed?'

'No . . . not particularly.'

'*Did* you notice?'

'No, sir.'

When one is asked questions again and again, one begins to doubt whether anything was so. This is something which has to be experienced to be understood. Dr Parnaby had given evidence, and had said it was understood that if Mr Webber woke in pain, he could be given a sleeping draught.

'You say you fell asleep yourself that afternoon?'

'Yes.'

'And you deny that you gave him any sleeping draught at all?'

'I gave him none. He was asleep all the time.'

'You fell asleep, and did not wake until the maid brought your tea?'

'That is correct.'

On and on went the questioning, circling and returning over and over again to the events of that afternoon. When the court adjourned temporarily, I felt so weak I was unable to walk without help. I was being cross-examined now — the hours and the days became indistinguishable.

'You were greatly shocked when your husband died, then, Mrs Webber?'

'Yes,' I whispered.

'And sorry? Deeply grieved?'

'I couldn't realize it at first,' I said.

'Did you nurse him with devotion?'

'To the best of my ability.'

'You had been married only a few months?'

'That is so.'

'And you loved your husband?'

At this point I faltered. The whole courtroom was silent, waiting for my reply.

'Will you please answer the question? This is something I must know. You are on oath to tell the truth. *Did* you love your husband?'

'Before we were married, I told him I did not think I loved him,' I said at last. 'He said this did not matter, as love for a woman came after marriage.'

'And did you grow to love him afterwards?'

I was silent; desperate.

'I could not help it if it did not come,' I said at last.

'You admit, then, that you did not love your husband?'

Again I hesitated.

'Did you love him?'

'No.'

A murmur ran through the crowded courtroom, but it was instantly and sternly quelled.

'But you loved his wealth?'

I did not reply.

'You knew that he was a wealthy man when you married him?'

'Yes.'

'And you knew that up to the time of his marriage to you, his cousin, Mr Herbert Webber, was his heir?'

'Yes.'

'Was your husband eager for a child?'

'I believe so.'

'And he was pleased when a child was expected?'

'He was very pleased.'

'And pleased with you, no doubt?'

'He was very happy about it,' I said.

'I put it to you that you persuaded your husband to make a new will as soon as you knew a child was expected.'

'I knew nothing of it,' I said.

'You were surprised, then, when the will was read?'

'Very surprised.'

'And you are surprised to know that you yourself are named as the heir, in default of any issue?'

'Yes.'

'Surprised that everything had been

altered so recently, and tied up very neatly, with you as chief beneficiary?'

'Yes.'

'I put it to you that you were not surprised at all. I put it to you that you schemed right from the start, knowing that your husband was infatuated.'

And so it went on; the endless questioning, the insinuations, the cruel assumptions. Half the time I felt in a stupor. As the trial dragged on, there never seemed to have been any other sort of life.

Only a crowded courtroom, and people looking at me. Several times during the hearing I collapsed, and had to be carried out of court. But all things end some time, and the day came, the terrible, dread day, when after the summing up, the jury went away to make their decision. Largely due to Dr Parnaby's evidence, the defence had suggested that, taking my condition into account, it was possible that I had woken up that afternoon, given my husband more laudanum that I should have, because I was not wide awake, and then gone to sleep again, and forgotten that I had.

Dr Parnaby had agreed that I was in a very worried state at the time, and very tired. He had said that he thought this was quite possible; in his experience as a medical man, he said, this sort of thing was not unknown.

'She is eighteen, and expects a child. Let justice be tempered with mercy,' said the judge, in his summing up. At last, the solemn-faced jury returned, having made their decision. I scarcely seemed to be part of the drama going on in that court.

'Maura Elizabeth Webber . . . not guilty of murder . . . guilty of criminal negligence . . . four years hard labour . . .'

Somebody broke into noisy weeping straight away. A great gasp seemed to go up from around me. And then there was blackness, and the sensation of being lifted up and carried away.

15

Women in prison ... strange, I had never even thought about it, in all my eighteen years. To be shut up in a cell; to be deprived of freedom, I who loved to feel a horse beneath me, and the fresh free air blowing around me. Birds chirping and building their nests; the first pale shoots of plants in the spring; green foliage of trees against the blue skies; summer scents; woodsmoke in the autumn, and the turn of the leaf. All the sights and sounds and smells which I had taken for granted; all were part of the free world, and no longer part of mine.

'You're free, Miss Maura, you're free!' Nellie's words came back mockingly. I had thought I was not free as Basil Webber's wife; how little I had known of real captivity. Now I was a prisoner to be constantly humiliated. The first horrifying reality was the cutting of my hair. Snip! Snip! With savage delight the wardress hacked unmercifully at my long, golden locks.

My own clothes were taken from me; I no longer felt a person, a human being. I was in a state of dazed shock. It was unbelievable that an innocent person could be treated like this.

If this could happen to me, then it could happen to others. How could I endure such treatment? But whatever happens to people, they go on thinking. Between weeping and praying, I tried again and again to remember what really happened that afternoon.

Had I actually given Basil an overdose of laudanum? And fallen asleep again, and obliterated it from my memory? Was it possible that someone could be guilty of doing this, and yet have no recollection?

Tossing in that hard, narrow bed, in that comfortless cell, these were the anguished thoughts that went through my mind.

And the child I was to bear — what was going to happen to it? On top of all this misery was the now far-off seeming, hopeless love between Charles Ancroft and myself. I seemed to have lived through a lifetime's experience in the space of a few months. But even in prison, life goes on. There was one comfort, one friend and one support throughout all this. Nellie.

Somehow she began to attend to my affairs while I was in gaol. When she visited me, she was able to tell me that Mr Redhead was seeing that everything was in order. She took permanent lodgings near the prison.

The money that I had inherited at such a cost did not help me a great deal. During the period of my pregnancy, I did not work as hard as I was expected to do afterwards, and it was possible to bribe one or two of the wardresses for additional favour.

Most of my fellow prisoners were wretchedly poor; creatures whose only solace in life when out of prison was the bottle. There were thieves, prostitutes and drunkards; women without hope, without friends, and with no homes to go to. Everywhere there was sickness; everywhere there was sadness; and throughout those long, terrible nights, cries of anguish could be heard coming from those wretched cells.

The effect of my imprisonment was terrible. I can remember feeling a sort of strange, frightening cheerfulness, during which time I laughed and sang.

Then I had a long spell of not speaking at all, of being scarcely aware of my surroundings. When Nellie visited me, I knew it was Nellie, but felt only indifference. I was aware of my bodily discomfort, though, and the fact that I was going to have a child.

Sometimes I used to dream of Charles, and wake up crying; sometimes I would have nightmarish dreams about that afternoon I spent in my husband's room. In my dream he would wake, and I would go to his bedside and give him the fatal dose of laudanum.

There were times when I could not distinguish between waking and sleeping, and then pain came, and blotted out everything. Pain such as I had never imagined could exist; an agony so terrible that I no longer felt human. There was neither day nor night, nor past nor future, only my cries of anguish, and my tortured body.

Eventually even the callously uncaring midwife became afraid; the prison surgeon appeared, angrily resentful. I floated away into an endless, sickly-smelling blackness . . .

When I came round, there was a tiny form beside me; still dazed with pain, I saw a face that was the miniature of Charles'.

The baby gave a feeble cry.

'It had better be baptized straight away,' came the prison surgeon's voice.

'Charles,' I managed to say, 'Charles . . .' Then I lost consciousness again.

The time that followed is very confused. Sometimes I slept, sometimes I woke. I could feel the wetness of perspiration trickling down the back of my neck; there was a great weakness which prevented me from even moving a limb. I seemed to be constantly drifting into unconsciousness, and drifting back.

My first clear memory during the time I was so ill, was of Nellie being with me.

'I've had a baby,' I said slowly.

'Yes, Miss Maura — a boy. They baptized him Charles, but he didn't live. Don't fret, things are better this way, far better. Get well and strong again. I must go now . . . ' Her voice faded away.

Slowly I regained a measure of health. As soon as I was able, I was put to work scrubbing floors, toiling in the laundry, and doing all the hard, disagreeable tasks imaginable in the prison; tasks which I had never dreamed my hands would have to do.

Some of the wardresses were impressed and slightly in awe, because they knew I had money, and was not the usual class of woman prisoner. In one or two cases I managed to ease my lot with bribery. As I was innocent, I saw no harm in this.

Other wardresses, however, were the opposite, and out of a sort of resentful envy, they heaped every humilation and degradation possible on me. After a while, all the past took on a dreamlike quality. The four walls of my cell became my home, and the wardresses, whether good or bad, were part of it.

At first, a few people who knew me were sympathetic; both Phyllis and Cassia were. But as time slipped by, they gradually lost interest; carried along no doubt by the bustling world outside, and the many other things which claimed their attention.

The one person who never failed me was Nellie, although I was often listless and apathetic during her short visits. She tried to bring me news of what was happening beyond the prison gates, but often, I did not want to know. It had been a cruel world to me, shutting me away, and turning its back on me when I was eighteen.

In winter, the prison was bitterly cold, and in summer the cell grew stifling. The prison chaplain told me to repent of my sins; that was the comfort I got from him.

But time passed, as time always passes. Months, and then years slipped by; the lost years of my girlhood. During the last few months of my captivity, a fever raged through the prison, causing sickness and death among prisoners and wardresses alike.

I fell victim, and for a long time I was very ill. Somehow I survived, due, I think, to the fact that what Nellie called 'a good foundation' had been laid during childhood.

And one wet day at the end of winter, weak and trembling and afraid, I left that grim building which had been my home for so long. The faithful Nellie, looking much older than when I had gone in, had a carriage waiting for me outside the prison gates.

I was barely convalescent. Heavily veiled, I walked outside those gates, a free woman at last. But I felt no happiness.

16

All these thoughts and memories passed through my mind the night I had seen Charles Ancroft again in that carriage, and fainted. The terrible shock of the past catching up with me, and so quickly, was too much to bear. And what would Charles want with me now? The girl he had known, that foolish, trusting girl, had gone forever. But he must have heard about me from somewhere — he must have known I was in Bath. Or was it just chance?

At last I fell asleep.

* * *

The following morning Liza, the maid, tapped on our sitting-room door, and entered. I was looking through the lace-curtained window onto the crescent below, and Nellie was crocheting a fine shawl.

'Yes, Liza?' I said.

'If you please, ma'am — ' she hesitated, and then the words came out with a rush. 'There is a manservant at the door with some flowers which he says are from his master, for you, Miss Hagan.'

For a moment I was quite unable to speak, then I burst out sharply — 'Tell him I do not receive flowers from gentlemen.'

'He said that his master said he was on no account not to deliver them, ma'am.'

'Oh, very well. You may take them and bring them up,' I said.

She left the room. Nellie paused in her crocheting, and glanced across.

'You know who they will be from — ' she began.

'Yes, Nellie, I know very well. Mr Ancroft is part of the past, and I don't wish to be reminded of it.'

'Miss Maura! He was so kind last night — and so helpful when you fainted — I cannot understand you.

Why should you not wish to renew your acquaintanceship with him? Why — '

'Nellie,' I said patiently, 'it was not an acquaintanceship — you know that. You brought me here to get a fresh start — to try and forget. Who can bring the past back more clearly that Charles Ancroft? Don't you understand — '

I broke off. It was hopeless; of course she could not understand. Liza knocked at the door again and I bade her enter. She was carrying a bouquet of daffodils and tulips; the flowers of spring.

I removed the envelope attached to them. Inside was a visiting card; the address was Royal Terrace, Bath. There was also a note.

'My dearest Maura' the note began. For a moment the words swam in front of me; bitter-sweet memories stirred; 'you cannot imagine my joy at seeing you after all this time. To be back in England after long years spent abroad is wonderful, but to see you again is better still. I am staying in Bath for an indefinite period, and I would be delighted if you would receive me. I shall call this afternoon at three o'clock'.

'Is the manservant waiting for a reply?' I asked Liza, as she arranged the flowers in a vase.

'No, ma'am.' She left the room. Nellie looked at me questioningly.

'He wishes to be received this afternoon,' I said.

'Oh! Miss Maura! And you will?'

'To revive memories which I would rather forget? It's so pointless and futile.'

For a moment Nellie did not speak, but crocheted in silence.

'Oh, very well,' I said at last. 'I will receive him — just this once.'

Her face brightened immediately. 'I've ordered the carriage for this afternoon, so I shall be out of the way.'

After luncheon, somewhat grudgingly, I looked in the wardrobe at some of the clothes which Nellie had had made for me. I picked out a dark grey dress, trimmed with contrasting bands of lilac velvet.

'I'll wear this, I think,' I said. Nellie

helped me into it, a pleased look on her face. It was a sober enough looking dress, but at least it was not black.

Some time later, the carriage she had ordered arrived. She went out, and I was left in the room alone. How quiet the house was — how quiet the crescent outside.

As I was looking through the window, the black brougham with the chestnut horses drew up outside. I certainly did not believe that Charles Ancroft had come to Bath by chance. I saw him step out of the carriage, and felt oddly detached. What was this handsome, elegantly dressed man coming to see me for? A few minutes later, Liza announced him, and I was alone with him for the first time in several years.

'Maura,' he said softly, and approached me with both hands outstretched. They clasped mine, and I was quite unable to speak. I stood there, breathless and trembling.

'It's been a long time.' His voice was husky with emotion. He was in his late twenties now; less boyish, but even more attractive than I remembered him. His presence brought fear, though. I wanted no more of men, for what had they brought me but unhappiness? We sat down, facing each other nervously.

'I hope you are well,' I said at last.

'*I* am well enough, Maura. It is you I am concerned about. An uncle of mine in Yorkshire died, and left me his entire estate. I decided to resign my commission.'

'And your brother?'

'You know he drank very heavily — well, things went from bad to worse. The end was bound to come sooner or later. It is not a pretty story.'

'No,' I said bitterly, 'and neither is mine.' What was the use of pretending? He must know what had happened to me.

'It was a long time before I heard about the trouble at Battle Tower. I never understood a lot of things.'

'Does it matter, now, anyway?' I asked. 'I just want to be left alone in peace.'

'Maura,' he said quietly, 'if I really believed that was what you wanted, then I would go away and leave you in peace. As it is, I've sought you out now that you are free. Whatever happened at Battle Tower, I am convinced that you were innocent of any blame — '

'I am not convinced of anything,' I said harshly. 'When a number of people decide that it is possible for you to do something, and that at the time you were not really responsible for your actions, you come to accept that you may have done it. I don't know.'

He changed the subject. 'I'm dreadfully sorry that I gave you such a shock last night. I realize now that making my presence known in such a way was not a good idea.'

'It would have been a shock if I had met you any other way.'

'Years ago,' he reminded me, 'I went to that cottage, and found a cruel note awaiting me. I dare not seek you out or do anything, because of the position you were in. I suffered torments — torments!

I was thankful to be posted overseas.'

'I did not write that note,' I said. 'I was not even allowed to write a farewell note to you! That note was written by Herbert Webber. He sent a note by a footman that morning, signed 'C', and naturally I thought it was from you. It told me to be at the cottage early that day — we hadn't even arranged to meet that day — but I went, as it said on the note that it was urgent — '

'Herbert Webber!'

'Yes. He was at the cottage waiting for me. It was a terrible shock. He threatened to tell my husband — he threatened me with all sorts — oh, it was abominable. I asked him to at least allow me to write a note to you myself, and he said only on his conditions.'

'His conditions?'

'Yes. Oh, can't you guess what they were?'

I saw sudden, incredulous anger in his eyes.

'And all this went on in that cottage?'

'Yes. It was terrible. But why talk

about it — why must I remember all that?'

'If I had known! If I could have been at that cottage when he was threatening you — ' He stood up, and paced restlessly round the room, as though even that activity gave his feelings some relief.

'If,' I said wearily. 'It's all 'if' in my life.'

He swung round abruptly. 'I'm not going to ask you a lot of painful questions about the past, Maura. I don't know how you feel towards me — towards anyone or anything now. I know you have not yet regained your health, and I'm not going to weary you.'

I said nothing, and he continued:

'Will you just give me the opportunity to see you — to visit you — arrange some outings — with Nellie in attendance, of course. All I ask is that you allow me to call.'

He sat down again in the chair opposite me, and leaned forward, his eyes earnest.

'Maura, will you allow me to be your friend?'

In spite of everything, I felt myself weakening.

'Oh ... very well,' I said at last. 'Although I cannot understand why you should still be interested in my welfare.'

'Don't try to understand anything. Just live from day to day, and enjoy the amenities of Bath. Are you comfortable here?'

'Very comfortable. We decided — well, I suppose it was Nellie who decided — that we would be better in quiet lodgings than in one of the big hotels.'

'I have leased a charming little house. You must come with Nellie to see it.'

'Bath is a fashionable place,' I said. 'There must be much to amuse and entertain you here.'

'There could be much to amuse and entertain you, Maura.'

For a while we talked; not about Wild Witton, nor Battle Tower, but mostly about Charles' career in the army where he had risen to the rank of captain, before resigning his commission.

I rang for Liza, and ordered tea. How strange it was to sit in that room, and pour tea for Charles Ancroft, and hand him dainty sandwiches and scones. It was almost like a dream, and yet it was so peaceful and pleasant that I felt I did not mind if it was a dream. My first shock and fear at seeing Charles had already passed. If this man who had come out of my past wanted no more than friendship, then perhaps there was no harm in granting it.

He took his leave shortly after tea, saying he did not wish to tire me. He added that with my permission he would call the following day with his carriage, and take Nellie and me out.

I was on the point of refusing, but he reminded me that I had already given my word that I would accept his friendship.

'Goodbye for now, Maura,' he said. 'The maid will see me out.'

He departed quite briskly, and with a

smile. From the window, I watched the smart carriage roll away, and shortly afterwards, Nellie returned from her drive.

'Well, Miss Maura?' She entered the room.

'Well, Nellie?'

She began to remove her outdoor clothes. 'Did Mr Ancroft call?'

'He did.'

I knew that she was bursting with curiosity.

'And you had a pleasant time?'

'We had a very nice conversation,' I said. 'Very well, I won't keep anything back from you. He asked if I would agree to regard him as a friend, and asked my permission to call here, and take us both for outings sometimes. In fact, he's calling here tomorrow afternoon, to take us driving.'

She looked pleased. 'I'm so glad. It's better to have a gentleman in attendance.'

17

The weeks that followed were quiet and tranquil. True to his word, Charles gave me his friendship, and asked for nothing else than to be allowed to call at the house and take Nellie and me driving, or on some other outing he had suggested.

We visited every place of interest in Bath. We took the waters; we went to concerts in the Pump Room. We strolled in the parks, and drove somewhere almost every day. Outside the town was beautiful countryside, it was hilly and wooded, with the gentle Avon flowing timelessly along. It was spring now, with the fragrance of blossoming fruit trees everywhere; the hedgerows were white with cow parsley, and the great chestnut trees heavy with candles.

As the spring turned into summer, and the heat in Bath became stifling, we quite often picnicked beside the river.

On one such occasion I remarked how peaceful the Avon looked.

'Yes. And yet it has overflowed and caused great havoc — and not very long ago,' said Charles. Nellie unpacked our picnic luncheon, and he opened a bottle of wine.

After our meal, which we ate in the shade of a sycamore tree, Charles asked if I would care to stroll along the banks of the river. It was almost deserted, save for one or two people fishing higher up. Charles and I walked along in silence. I had replaced my bonnet and veil, which I had removed while we ate our meal.

I also carried a pale blue parasol. The scent of wild flowers rose up on all sides; how lush and green this part of England was.

I stumbled, and Charles slipped his arm through mine. To my surprise, I caught my breath at the contact.

We stopped walking.

'Why are you carrying a parasol, Maura?'

'Well . . . to keep the sun off, I suppose.'

'What sun do you suppose can get at

you, all dressed up in that long-sleeved black outfit, with that bonnet and veil? You look like some old lady, come to Bath to spend her few remaining years.'

'I'm sorry you don't approve of my clothes,' I said stiffly, after a pause.

'Approve of them? How on earth could I? I think — '

'Don't you think you are presuming on our friendship?'

'I don't really care what I am presuming on. Do you know who you remind me of?'

I was silent.

'I'll tell you, then. You remind me of Basil Webber's first wife — the unfortunate woman who wore a veil all the time — just like you do. Indeed, I am surprised you don't wear in it the house, like she apparently did. We are alone on the river bank. Take it off.'

As I was feeling somewhat indignant and startled at his attitude, I refused to do this. With a sudden movement he untied the ribbons, and removed it himself.

'That's better. The gold is coming

back into your hair, Maura.'

I gave a gasp, as the next moment my bonnet flew through the air, and landed in the Avon.

'How dare you throw my bonnet in the river?' I was utterly taken by surprise at his gesture. 'I don't want anyone to see my face.'

'Why not? It's a beautiful face, but it's too sad.'

I was still somewhat taken aback by his attitude. But now the black bonnet was just a small speck on the river. I looked at it, slowly disappearing out of sight. Charles burst out laughing. He gave my hand a little squeeze, and released it. Rather to my surprise I began to laugh too.

'Promise you'll buy some new clothes?'

'Nellie did have some made,' I admitted. 'But I wouldn't wear them — except for a grey dress which I've worn in the house. Well, I'll think about it.' We strolled slowly back to where Nellie was sitting.

'Why, where is your bonnet?' were her first words.

'Floating down the Avon,' said

Charles with a smile.

Nellie looked startled for a moment; then she too smiled. No more mention was made of the bonnet. Back in Chippenham Crescent, though, I looked at myself in the mirror with renewed interest. My cheeks were growing rounded and pink again, and, yes, the gold was coming back into my hair. I turned round to Nellie.

'Help me off with this dress,' I said. Without a word, she did so. 'And help me on with the blue silk one.'

Minutes later I stood in the gown she'd had made for me so hopefully a few months before.

'Well,' I said, 'how do I look?'

'You look — like Miss Maura,' said Nellie simply.

I twirled round in front of the mirror. Could I truly face going around without being veiled — without appearing an inconspicuous woman in mourning?

'I feel strange in pretty gowns,' I said slowly. 'Mr Ancroft threw my bonnet into the river. I know I laughed, but it was impertinent of him.'

'That's a matter of opinion. As Mr Ancroft is devoting so much time and attention to you, don't you think it would be very nice for you and for him if you dressed fashionably, in becoming clothes?'

'Oh, well, I'll think about it. Why, Nellie, what is wrong?'

She had gone very pale. Indeed, her face looked drawn with pain.

'What is wrong?' I repeated.

'It's nothing,' she said, rubbing her side briskly. 'I'll be all right if I sit and rest for a while. Perhaps the sun was too hot for me.'

'You had better rest,' I said. I felt afraid. Nellie had always seemed immortal to me. She rarely complained of anything connected with her health, but the past few years must have been a strain for her. Was this clinging to mourning and a veil a form of self-indulgence on my part?

It would certainly please her if I discarded it.

'Oh, well,' I said briskly. 'I won't wear black any more, Nellie.'

She smiled faintly, but I sensed she was still in pain.

'It's probably indigestion,' I said, and rang the bell for Liza to bring her something to relieve it.

Later on she seemed to improve, and I read to her a little before we retired.

That day seemed to mark a turning point for me. I went out of the house no longer veiled, nor dressed in black. Admiring glances soon began to come my way. They did not go unnoticed by Charles.

'I had more peace of mind when you were veiled,' he said one day. He was smiling, though. It was a day when he received me alone in the house he had leased in Royal Terrace. By Battle Tower standards it was tiny, but it had a charm all its own.

Charles had a small but very good domestic staff. Nellie was supposed to have been accompanying me that day, as we were to dine there, and then attend a concert. She had pleaded a headache, though. I sat in the small, but tastefully furnished drawing room, and looked out at the park beyond. I still found this freedom strange; I would sometimes glance fearfully behind me when I was out walking. Charles sat down opposite me.

'No wonder men look at you,' he remarked. 'Maura, it's so wonderful that we are together again. I shan't ever let you go.'

'But Charles, it's impossible — ' I broke off. Just sitting in the same room with him, feelings which I had thought lost for ever began to stir within me.

Married in the sight of God! We had taken those vows in the madness of our passion for each other, one autumn day when I was a girl of eighteen. As our eyes met, I knew that he was thinking of it too.

'I've put . . . all that sort of thing out my life, Charles,' I stammered.

'Don't talk such nonsense! I've never pressed you to tell me all the facts before, but don't you think you should, now? After we have dined . . . haven't we wasted enough time — missed enough happiness? Do you think that after all these years — after leaving the army and finding you again — do you think I am going to walk out of your life, and let you go on moping for ever?'

'But Charles, when you know all the facts, you may think differently,' I said. 'You may not think me a fit woman to — to —'

'Are you going to say 'to marry'? My dearest Maura, of course I want to marry you; I want to make up to you for everything. I want to enfold you in my love. You can't stand in the way of your own happiness.'

'With a past like mine — with a shadow over my life such as I have had — things which other women cannot even imagine? Sometimes in the night I wake in fear. And you cannot marry a woman who would be pointed out. I would not be received in society, you must know that, Charles.'

281

'Do you think I care a jot about such things? There is no regiment to think about now.'

Dinner was served, simply, but tastefully, in the pleasant dining room. Afterwards we again sat in the drawing room together.

'How nice to have a little Georgian house like this to come to,' I said impulsively. 'Small, but possessing everything necessary for — ' I paused.

'For what?'

'Oh . . . happiness, I suppose.'

'Happiness . . . yes. Now, Maura, will you tell me everything that happened to you from our last meeting in that cottage in the grounds of Battle Tower? However painful it is, tell me. And try and remember everything.'

Slowly at first, and with much hesitation, I found myself recounting the whole story. Charles did not interrupt me very often, although occasionally when I fell silent, he prompted me. Perhaps one of the most painful parts was telling him about those first few months in prison.

'A son was born. He was our son, Charles. He was like you. He died, though, shortly after birth. I remember little about it,' I said.

'Our son? Oh, Maura! You had our child — in prison!'

The horror and anguish on his face brought the memory back all too vividly.

'Please don't talk about it. It is past,' I said. I could see that Charles was upset by what I had told him, but he controlled himself, and I continued talking. When I had finished, he asked me to tell him again what Herbert Webber had said when the will was being read. He looked very thoughtful.

'It all sounds very suspicious to me. Herbert Webber cared nothing for his cousin, from what you say. Had the will remained with him the heir, I doubt if he would have queried the way his cousin died at all.'

'He wouldn't,' I said. 'Nor would he if I had consented to marry him after the reading of the will. But how could I foresee the consequences of an inquiry into my husband's death? And even if I could, how could I have married Herbert Webber? Charles, don't you see, there has never been anything I could do, other than I have, from the time I became Basil Webber's wife?'

He nodded sympathetically.

'You were little more than a child, and you were a victim of circumstances — just as I was. I felt my brother had betrayed our birthright by selling Battle Tower to Basil Webber, and yet, there was nothing I could do, as the younger brother. I went into the army. And Michael gave me scarcely anything; a pittance. My hands were tied. There was nothing I could do, or offer you, Maura, except my love. And I was so afraid for you. It was an impossible situation.'

For a moment we both sat thinking. Then Charles leaned forward, and clasped my hand in his. 'But there is nothing to stop us marrying now. I love you, Maura.'

I knew that I had to be strong; that if I gave way to my feelings I would agree to marry Charles, and by doing so I would ruin his life. I fought against a desire to nestle in his arms.

'Charles, I can't marry you! For your sake — don't you see?'

He released my hand. 'You mean because of what other people think — when I have told you I care nothing of what they think?'

'Partly.'

'But you still care for me?'

I turned away to hide the sudden tears. 'Yes, I care,' I whispered. 'It's not being certain myself. Did I do that terrible thing — and yet have no recollection of doing it at all?'

'I suppose you were pretty distraught at the time. But it still seems very odd to me that Herbert Webber never mentioned anything before the will was read. I suppose everyone was questioned, and could more or less say where they were that afternoon?'

'Yes. They all seemed to give

satisfactory stories.'

'I understand Herbert Webber is abroad,' went on Charles. 'In fact, I believe he is living in Ravenna. I could soon find out.'

'What use would that be?'

He walked restlessly over to the window. 'I'd like a talk with Herbert Webber. In fact, I'd like a talk with a few people concerning your husband's death. If any fresh evidence comes to light, you could ask for a re-trial. And even if it doesn't — well, I would still like to see Webber.'

'I couldn't stand a re-trial,' I said. 'I couldn't stand anything like that.'

'We won't talk about it any more now.' Charles sat down at the piano. 'Come, Maura, we have time for one song before we go out. You sing, and I'll play.'

'Sing!' I said. 'I haven't sung for years.'

'Then it's high time you did. And it's high time, too, that you started to mix with people other than Nellie and myself.'

'What people? I couldn't mix — '

'It's all you couldn't, you couldn't, Maura! Try saying, I can — I can! I haven't bothered much with Bath society, but I do know a number of people here; some permanent residents, some just here for the season.'

'People would be too curious about me, Charles. They would want to know who I was, and where I came from. Oh, no, it would be unthinkable!'

'Not at all. I have already put it about that I have a distant relation staying in Bath. A young lady from Ireland. Not strictly true, perhaps, but it's a very white lie. Between us we will make up a good, watertight background for you, and you can enter into some social life. After all, you *were* a relation, distant from me for a long time — my wife — in the sight of God! Remember?'

Again the poignant memories of our exchanged vows stirred in me, and the way Charles spoke made me realize he had no intention of allowing me to forget. I wanted to protest; to say that it was too much to expect me to meet people in Bath. I wanted to say that he had no right to . . . no right to . . .

But somehow, the protests died unspoken. He had a very determined look on his face. It made me realize how much he must have suffered when younger, to see his feckless brother selling Battle Tower over his head, and yet be unable to do anything. And how he must have suffered over my marriage, and yet again, he could do nothing.

He rippled the piano keys, and glanced across at me, smiling his wide, sweet smile, which chased the sudden, soldier hardness from his face. 'Drink to me only with thine eyes, Maura,' he said.

18

Not long after this conversation, through Charles' influence, I was invited with him for a musical evening at a Mr and Mrs Tripp's house. It was a pleasant, Georgian house, built on a hill overlooking Bath. From the drawing room we had an excellent view of the wonderful, spreading crescents below.

'Ah, yes, Miss Hagan,' said Mr Tripp. 'Here we can look down on one of the few cities in Europe designed as a city — designed to be beautiful. When the rain-mist covers it, it is not at its best, but as it is tonight, with the setting sun turning to fire on the stonework, and the abbey standing out above all other buildings . . . ' He paused. 'But I believe you have some beautiful architecture in Ireland, have you not?'

'Oh, indeed, yes,' I said, in some confusion. The night was warm, and I fanned myself vigorously. Where was Charles? Deep in conversation with the Tripps' eldest daughter, Philippa. I was was very nervous of the assembled company. Suppose the conversation should turn to things of which I was ignorant, due to being cut off from society so long?

'You must make a friend of Philippa, my dear,' said the genial Mr Tripp. 'Young ladies are independent these days. You are living in rooms in Bath, I understand, with a companion?'

'Yes, sir.' My voice was almost inaudible.

'And why not, indeed? I'm sure Mr Ancroft is only too pleased to show you all the places of interest. Cousins can be very useful, very useful indeed, to young ladies.'

He was a portly, pleasant man. His wife was tall, thin and fashionably dressed. She clearly wanted to impress people; her eyes darted round the assembled company, taking in every detail of every lady's apparel. She had a habit of referring to 'the dear Queen' as if she were on close terms with her.

Suddenly I knew why Charles had been invited, even though I was there too. He had been there before; he had told me that. The Tripps were hoping for a match for their daughter, Philippa. She was about nineteen, and as they had three younger daughters, they probably thought the sooner she was settled, the better.

Charles was a good pianist, and as he played, she sang in a sweet and tuneful soprano. We applauded with enthusiasm, and Philippa blushed. Although not pretty, in the softly fading light of a summer evening, she looked attractive. My first feelings of fear and shyness seemed to leave me, and were replaced by another, stronger emotion. How handsome Charles looked, his white shirt and dark suit showing off his summer tan to advantage.

He was laughing at something Philippa had said, and I found myself resenting her being so close to him;

resenting, too, the approving look on her mother's face.

They need not consider him a suitable match for their daughter. He was mine! Somebody played the violin; supper was served, but as the evening went on, I found my jealousy steadily growing.

By the time we had taken our leave of the Tripps, and I was in the carriage with Charles, I could barely speak.

'I trust you enjoyed the evening,' he said.

'I'm sure *you* did.'

'I? Well, it was quite pleasant. But the best part was seeing you mixing with other company — and you appeared quite at ease, too.'

'*You* were certainly at ease.'

'What is wrong? Oh — I see!' He burst out laughing, which annoyed me still further. 'Don't you like me accompanying Miss Philippa when she sings?'

'Why should I mind? You are at liberty to please yourself.'

'Maura! Don't spoil the evening

— don't have such foolish thoughts. I can assure you, I have no romantic ideas in connection with Miss Tripp, much as I esteem her. The Tripps are a pleasant family, and quite well thought of in Bath. Remember, at the moment, Bath is your home, and mine, too. You cannot skulk away for the rest of your life. If you mix with people, and become accepted in Bath society, that is a tremendous step forward. The fact that we are presumed to be distant cousins means we can be seen in each other's company without arousing unpleasant gossip. You are merely considered a very modern young lady of independent means, in rooms with a companion. Undoubtedly, knowing the Tripps can open many doors in Bath. As for Philippa — think no more of that. There must be many suitors for that young lady.'

I was not so sure of that, however, I put my jealous thoughts out of my mind as much as possible. About this time, the son of the house, Edgar, came home from abroad, where he had been on business. Although the Tripps lived in some style, and Mrs Tripp thought a great deal of herself, nevertheless, Mr Tripp had business interests in Bristol, connected with coffee. Because of this, Edgar, who was about the same age as Charles, often went abroad on his father's behalf.

He had a good appearance, being tall and fair; a younger edition of his father, in fact, and with the same cheerful manner.

'Delighted to meet you, Miss Hagan. Delighted,' he beamed, bowing over my hand when we were introduced. And it became apparent in a very short time that he really was delighted to meet me.

Edgar and his sister, and Charles and I began to make up a foursome, chaperoned by either his mother or Nellie. We went to concerts and the theatre; even to one or two balls. I was sure that things were getting too much for Nellie, though. She often seemed tired, although she did not complain. I noticed with some concern that she appeared to be getting steadily thinner.

'Might you settle in Bath for good? Your cousin told me you had been ill, and you came here in the first place to convalesce,' remarked Edgar Tripp one evening, when we were attending a concert in the Pump Room.

'Yes, that is true,' I murmured somewhat nervously. It was the interval, and as usual, Edgar tried to have a private conversation with me, something which I always sought to avoid. Both his parents were with us that evening. I was wearing a rather unusual gown of amber-coloured silk, trimmed with cream lace.

Mr and Mrs Tripp recognized a couple they knew in the audience; a Mr and Mrs Braithwaite. They were middle-aged, and were staying in Bath with Mrs Braithwaite's sister, who was a friend of Mrs Tripp, and that was how they had met them in the first place. The Braithwaites did not belong to Bath.

When Mrs Tripp introduced us, Mrs Braithwaite appeared to be looking very hard at Charles.

'Why it isn't — it can't be — yes, you must be! An Ancroft from the Border country . . . you once lived at Battle Tower, surely? You were just a boy in those days — too busy with your own affairs to notice all the older people who visited. And it must be years now . . . yes, that very wealthy man bought it from your brother . . . what was his name? Ah, I remember — Webber. Came to a sticky end, didn't he? I suppose you know — '

We were just leaving the Pump Room after the concert. I had not yet been intoduced. I caught my breath with shock at her words, and Edgar put his hand under my arm.

'And this is Miss Maura Hagan — Mr and Mrs Braithwaite — Miss Hagan, are you feeling quite well?'

His voice was anxious. Mrs Braithwaite turned her eager gaze on me. 'Hagan?' she began, but her husband interposed hastily.

'It was rather warm in there,' he said

smoothly. 'I'm sure it's delightful to meet old friends again. Undoubtedly we will see you all again during our stay in Bath.' He bowed hurriedly, and appeared to be ushering his rather too talkative wife out of the way as soon as possible.

Charles' anxious gaze met my eye. There was a slight constraint about our party as we got into the waiting carriages. We had not planned to break up straight away, but Charles said I did not feel very well, and it might be wise to take me back to Chippenham Crescent straight away. Edgar said he was most anxious, and that he would call on me the next morning, to see how I was.

Once in the carriage alone with Charles, I found I was trembling violently.

'Charles, I am certain that Mrs Braithwaite knew my name,' I said. 'I should have chosen another name altogether — not gone back to Hagan. I thought I was safe enough — '

297

'You are safe enough. I am sure that even if Mrs Braithwaite remembers things, she will keep quiet.' He slipped his arm through mine reassuringly. Suddenly my fear turned to other emotions. The passions of my girlhood, scarcely roused before they were crushed down for years, rose in me, as fiercely as ever.

And I had thought that part of my life was over! I pressed his arm close to me. That gesture was enough for Charles; the next moment I felt his lips on mine, eager, passionate.

Locked in each other's arms we sat in the carriage, oblivious of everything. The luminous blue of the west country sky had deepened into starlit dusk; the streets were quiet save for the clip-clop of the horses' hooves. The rest of the world faded out; this was my world; a tiny, enclosed world, where only Charles Ancroft mattered, and the words he was whispering, and the pressure of his lips on mine.

'I love you, Maura, my darling! As much as ever — more, in fact. I want to marry you. Put the past to one side and become my wife.'

We went on kissing, with the blind, passionate urgency of lovers long parted.

'We *must* get married, Maura. We can't go on like this. It's an impossible situation.'

'But don't you see, I can't. It would not be fair to you — '

'Do you think this is fair to me? Oh, don't let's talk about it now. Not tonight. Tomorrow we will talk.'

Again he clasped me in his arms, and we remained in a close embrace until the carriage drew up outside Mrs Marchbanks' house in Chippenham Crescent.

19

I slept little that night, and was glad to rise the following morning. I found Nellie to be far from well, and tried to persuade her to have the doctor.

'I shall be quite well if I rest, Miss Maura,' she said obstinately. She remained in bed, and I made my toilet without her help. Later in the morning, Edgar Tripp called. Looking extremely nervous, he sat down and cleared his throat.

'Miss Hagan, there is something I must say to you. I know it may seem rather sudden, but believe me, I have given the matter a great deal of thought — '

He stood up and moved towards me. I had been afraid of this.

'You do like me, Miss Hagan?'

'Why — yes, of course, as a friend.'

'I am content with that at present.

Well, not content, perhaps, but I am prepared to wait if you are not ready for a formal proposal yet. I would wait years if necessary . . . if you could just give me a little hope.'

I knew that he had been getting fond of me, but this was yet another complication. I could not help the cynical thought crossing my mind that his love would die a swift death if he knew of my past. I managed to retain my composure, though. His eager hands clasped mine; I drew away gently.

'You do me a great honour,' I said quietly. 'I must be honest with you, though. I can give you no hope.'

For a moment he looked quite stricken. His face paled.

'None at all, Miss Hagan?'

'None at all. I'm sorry.'

He sat down again. 'Very well. I have not given up hope, but I shall not mention it again — not for some time, anyway. I trust we will continue to be friends?'

'Of course we will.'

Later that day Charles called to see me, and I told him about Edgar's proposal. He was not pleased.

'Now that you are mixing in society again, this sort of thing is bound to happen. Maura, you are standing in the way of your own happiness — and mine. We have wasted enough time. We must get married.'

'But don't you see, Charles, I have this shadow hanging over me. It simply would not be fair. No, I can never marry.'

'I've mentioned this before, Maura. I'm not satisfied with a lot of things about your trial. I suspect foul play, and I've a good idea where it came from, too. I intend to look into this matter. I'm going to find Herbert Webber. If necessary, I'll hunt him to the ends of the earth.'

I could see that he was absolutely determined.

'But . . . I shall be alone if you go away, Charles.'

'You and Nellie must move into the

house I am leasing here. You know I have a good domestic staff — you would be very comfortable. You could live there quietly during my absence.'

'I should hate being without you,' I said quickly. 'Please don't leave me, Charles.'

'What must I do, then? As matters stand you won't marry me. I fully believe your husband was given an overdose of sleeping draught on purpose. If I take the matter up again — if anything comes to light through my investigations, would you be prepared for a re-trial?'

'I don't know. It's so difficult — '

'But you won't marry me, Maura! Can't you see it's up to you to do your part, too? It's only fair to me.' Impetuously he reached forward, and once again I experienced the rapturous joy of feeling his arms around me, his lips pressed on mine. We belonged together, and we both knew it.

'Very well,' I said at last. 'But if you try — and find nothing — what then?'

'Then either you marry me, or we must part, Maura. How else would you have things?'

'I don't know,' I said helplessly. How could I bear to see him go out of my life a second time? How could I marry him though, and ruin his life? The past was always with me.

'Nellie is ill,' I said, changing the subject. 'She seems to be in pain. She's been in bed today, but she refuses to see the doctor. I'm so worried about her, Charles.'

'What nonsense! Won't see a doctor — of course she must have the doctor if she is unwell. Can't you send the maid for him? Never mind, I'll attend to it myself.'

Nellie had proved so obstinate about this that I was extremely glad that Charles was taking responsibility in this matter. She had lost a lot of weight over the past few months, and I had an uneasy feeling that she was often in pain. Nevertheless I had some trepidation when I entered her room to tell her

Dr Rice was being summoned. A fresh pang of fear struck me when I saw how ill she looked.

'Are you no better, Nellie?' I asked, hurrying to her bedside. She shook her head, forcing a faint smile.

'Mr Ancroft has gone for the doctor.'

To my surprise, she did not object.

'Nellie, he is eager for me to marry him,' I went on.

'I'm so glad,' she said quietly.

'I can't, though. It's an impossible situation. I could not possibly marry him after what has happened in the past. He says he is determined to get to the bottom of what really happened at Battle Tower. He believes that the fatal dose of laudanum was given quite deliberately by someone and he says he will find out who it was, however long it takes him. And if he finds anything, he wants a re-trial.'

Nellie said nothing. She must have been in pain; her face was haggard, with a yellowish tinge.

'You must get better, Nellie,' I went

305

on. 'Mr Ancroft wants us both to live in his house here, while he is making inquiries.'

'Why let him go to all that trouble?' she asked at last, her fingers picking nervously at the bedcover. 'Why don't you just marry him as soon as possible, Miss Maura? What does it matter now, anyway? It is past.'

I walked over to the window. The scene outside was autumnal; brown leaves were blowing in heaps along the crescent. Soon it would be winter. As I looked a dogcart came briskly along, and Dr Rice alighted from it. He must have come with all speed.

'Dr Rice is here now, Nellie,' I said, forcing myself to sound cheerful. I smoothed her bedcover, reflecting that only a few months before, I had been the patient. I left the doctor alone with Nellie, and went into our sitting room. My thoughts were in a whirl as I sat in front of the fire. The clock ticked on, and I seemed to have sat there for ever. At last the door opened, and the doctor appeared. His face was grave, and I was struck by a fear so terrible that I found myself rooted to the chair. He cleared his throat.

'Well, Miss Hagan, I'm afraid it's not good news about your companion. She is extremely ill, and will require skilled nursing.'

He paused a moment, before continuing. 'She must have been concealing the true state of her health for some time. There is a very good nursing home in Bath, which I can recommend. It is impossible for her to stay here, you understand. She must have attention from a proper nursing staff.'

For a moment I thought I was going to faint. My mouth went dry. When my voice came, it sounded far away and hoarse.

'And if she goes into this nursing home, and has skilled attention, how long will it be before she gets well?'

Dr Rice seemed to be searching for the right words to say. He patted my shoulder gently.

'You must brace yourself for this, Miss Hagan. She will not get well at all. A few weeks; that is all I can give. But she must not be told. Be cheerful, be optimistic, but make it clear to her that she must go into a nursing home.'

I was too stunned at the time to weep, which was just as well. Although the rest of the day was unreal, somehow, I maintained a cheerful manner, and told Nellie calmly that the doctor thought it best for her to enter a nursing home. To my surprise, she took it just as calmly. It crossed my mind that she had already guessed what the doctor had told me in confidence.

Charles called again that evening, and I told him what the doctor had said. Alone with him, I was unable to hold back my tears any longer. The seemingly inevitable loss of Nellie, whose strength had sustained me since childhood, seemed quite unbearable.

'We've gone through so much together,' I sobbed. 'She is not really old yet. She helped me to recover from those awful

years of imprisonent, and now, when she could enjoy life without worry — now — '
I was unable to continue.

Charles kissed my tears, and held me close without speaking for a while. 'At least, she has lived to see you free, and in good health,' he pointed out. 'Try thinking, not how tragic things are, but how much worse they could have been, for Nellie and for you.'

For the next few weeks I put my own problems to one side, faced with the tremendous fact of Nellie's illness. She was moved to the Avon Nursing Home, a gracious Georgian house on the fringes of the city. The Tripps soon knew of Nellie's illness, and were sympathetic, particularly Edgar. He said no more about his feelings towards me, but remained solicitous and friendly, for which I was grateful.

One raw, damp afternoon, Nellie seemed very much better, almost animated. Her eyes were sunken in her wasted face, but they looked with unusual eagerness at Charles and me when we arrived at the nursing home.

'Why, Nellie,' I exclaimed, kissing her, 'you look much better.'

'Yes, I feel I am improving,' she said cheerfully. Charles kissed her too, and gave her a bouquet of hot-house roses. Before we left her, she expressed a wish to see him alone. I was very much surprised, and so was he.

'There are things I want to talk over with him,' she explained. 'I might need a solicitor.'

'Of course I'll come along, if that is what you wish,' said Charles. 'I'll come tomorrow, and bring a solicitor, if you like.'

As we drove home through the gloom of a winter afternoon, he said she probably wanted to put her affairs in order, and that he thought it a very good idea.

'I still don't know why she wants just you,' I said.

'Perhaps she simply doesn't want to bother you. Dearest, if I can be of any service to Nellie, I'm only too pleased, at a time like this. Just rest tomorrow, and I will call round in the evening.'

I spent the following day quietly. In the evening, Liza dressed my hair for me, a service which her mistress did not object to. In a strange, unexpected sort of way, Mrs Marchbanks was, if not a friend, a person very kindly disposed towards me.

She considered me 'gentry', and she was very jealous of the reputation of her house, like most of her friends and acquaintances in the crescent. She often said that if her husband had lived, she would never have had to let rooms to people, a statement which was probably true.

The fire burned cheerfully in the hearth; the curtains were drawn against the unpleasantness of the winter evening, and I sat staring pensively into the glowing coals, waiting for Charles. When Liza announced him, I stood up eagerly.

To my surprise he came slowly forward, his face serious.

'Well?' I asked.

He took me in his arms and held me for a long time, very closely and tenderly.

'Nellie?' I asked at last, my voice a strangled whisper. 'Is she — ?'

'I have seen the doctor. He does not think she has very much longer to live.'

'Oh . . . ' I was silent, trembling in his arms. 'And does she know this? Did she want to see you to put her affairs in order?'

'In a manner of speaking. Yes.'

He pushed me gently down into a chair, and drew another one up beside it.

'Will we be undisturbed, Maura?'

'Well — yes, up to eight o'clock. I've asked for a supper tray to be sent up then.'

Something in his manner was so strange that I was filled with apprehension.

'What's wrong, Charles?' I asked. 'Is there something apart from Nellie's illness?'

He leaned forward and clasped my hands.

'She wants us to be married as soon as possible. It is her wish.'

'But — but — she knows the reasons why I feel I cannot. And before she went into the nursing home, I told her you wanted to make inquiries concerning my husband's death.'

'Precisely. That was why she wanted to see me.'

'I don't understand,' I said slowly.

'She doesn't want me to make these inquiries, darling.'

'I know that. She said it was the past, and over and done with.'

'Yes, but there is more to it than that, Maura.'

'How do you mean?'

'It is no longer necessary to make any inquiries. Nellie knows who did it, and she has told me.'

'Nellie knows? Nellie knows?' My voice rose incredulously. 'How could she know? If she had known, do you think she would have let me endure what I did? Why, Charles, she must be rambling — '

'Maura, my dearest! She is not rambling. Prepare yourself for a shock . . . Nellie gave Basil Webber the overdose herself.'

In the light of the oil lamp, I stared at him without comprehension. I felt numb of all feeling. This nonsense he was talking . . . nonsense, it was outrageous. I tried to push his hands away.

'It is true, Maura,' he said quietly.

Suddenly the shadows in the room seemed to grow bigger and bigger, enveloping me as I sat there. I tried to speak, to tell him how ill I was feeling, but the shadows all became one; I heard my voice crying out in anguish and disbelief against what seemed to me the ultimate, terrible betrayal of my life.

When I came round, I was shaken by sobs. Mrs Marchbanks was in the room with Charles; she was holding smelling salts under my nose.

'A hot drink is what she needs. I'll have the supper tray prepared immediately, Mr Ancroft.'

'Thank you, Mrs Marchbanks. This illness of her companion's is such a strain.'

I heard the door close behind her imposing figure. Charles knelt before me, and clasped my hands.

'Maura, dearest Maura, I know it is a terrible shock — I could not believe it at first, either. But I have a statement, sworn by her, signed by her, witnessed by the solicitor and me. She has confessed, and wants your forgiveness.'

'My forgiveness!' I sobbed, my voice growing hysterical. 'Forgiveness! How can I forgive? You don't understand what I have suffered — it is impossible to make anyone understand such things. I have been through a living hell because of her! Oh, God, it is unendurable — '

'Maura, please, please, will you listen to me? Calm down, my dearest.'

Charles dabbed my eyes gently with his handkerchief, but still the tears came. I was shivering. He plied the poker in the fire, until a fierce blaze sprang up. A part of me refused to believe what he was saying, but another part of me knew that he was speaking the truth.

'She says she came into the room that afternoon unseen by anyone. You were asleep in the chair. She said she saw tears on your cheeks, Maura, and she could not bear your unhappiness any longer. Your husband was awake, but very quiet. She poured out the fatal dose, and gave him it. Then she settled him down, and crept out. She said it was an impulse, and having done it, she thought it would remain undiscovered. The trouble was, she did not really think of the possible consequences at the time. She merely thought to free you from a husband she knew you were unhappy with. Dearest, she is not a clever woman; she loves you; she felt strongly that you had been a victim of cruel circumstances. Wills, inheritances; things like that she knew little about. She thought that you were sure to be well provided for as the widow of a rich man. Then, when the will was read, and Herbert Webber voiced his suspicions, she panicked. She was just not brave enough to confess to what she had done. Naturally, she never dreamed suspicion would fall on you — never dreamed you would be charged with his murder. When you got off with a few year's imprisonment, it was a great relief to her. She moved where she could be near to you, and cared for you as best she could — with loving devotion — '

'She did that — to me,' I said slowly, my body still shaken with sobs. 'She let me take the blame for what she did! I can never forgive her — never! How could she see me imprisoned, and know I was innocent?' After the first shock, I was gripped with a terrible, burning anger.

'I never want to see her again,' I said.

'But Maura, she is a dying woman now. She's paid for her crime through her own suffering as well as yours. Show her some pity. Don't judge her too harshly, I beg of you. When I resigned my commission and returned to England, I made inquiries as to your whereabouts, and the solicitor put me in touch with Nellie.'

'Oh,' I said. 'You never told me the details before of how you traced me

. . . so everything was arranged between you and Nellie?'

'Maura — please! Nellie agreed to meet me, and we discussed your situation, and she thought it was best for me not to make myself known to you while you were still in prison. But she said she would let me know when you were to be released, and where she would take you to recover from it all. I said I would go wherever she took you, and take up our acquaintanceship again, and I did. Dearest, she knows she did an appalling thing, giving your husband an overdose, and then letting you take the blame for it. She thought you would have married me, and put the past behind you. Don't you see, Maura, it's taking courage to do what she is doing now?'

'I never want to see her again,' I repeated.

Charles said nothing for a while. His face was drawn and tired. He lifted my hands to his lips, and kissed them, very tenderly.

'Don't be too harsh, Maura. You may see things very differently in a few months' time. But by then it will be too late.'

'Suppose she wasn't ill,' I said. 'What would have happened then? Would she have confessed in any case? Did you ask her that?'

'No, I didn't. Oh, Maura, it's never any use thinking like that. Nellie is dying; she is attempting to make reparation. She did wrong, yes, but she dearly wants you to marry me and be happy. The most wonderful thing is that we have each other — don't you see?'

At this point Liza appeared with a large tray. She looked at me with concerned eyes as she set the table for two.

'Is there anything else, ma'am? Are you recovered?' she asked before leaving.

'Yes, tell Mrs Marchbanks Miss Hagan is much better now. There is nothing else, Liza,' said Charles.

She bobbed a little curtsey and withdrew.

'Now I know you're going to say

you're not hungry,' he continued. 'But you must at least have some soup. I'm not very hungry either. We must have *something*, though.'

He served some soup from the small tureen, and coaxed me into having some. I also tried to eat a lamb cutlet, although it seemed as if it were choking me. Even though my first feelings of anger had calmed a little, I felt a sense of outrage so intense that it almost frightened me.

It seemed to swamp all other feelings. I could still scarcely believe that this woman who had cared for me throughout most of my life, who had shared my joys and sorrows, and had all my trust, could have stood to one side and let me be imprisoned for something which she herself had done.

'Would you rather I left?' asked Charles, gently. 'If you would prefer to be alone to think things over, then I will go.'

'Why couldn't she at least have told me this herself?' I asked bitterly. 'Why did she have to tell you?'

'I have no doubt, dearest, that she thought it would come better from me. Maura, with your permission, I think I will go now. I feel that I cannot do any good just now, after telling you the facts. I can only say, try to get some rest tonight. I know it must be terrible for you, to have to adjust to this. You know I feel deeply for you, and for your suffering. But think how Nellie must have suffered too; remorse, guilt, fear; she told me it was a tremendous relief to tell someone at last.'

A short while later, Charles left. He held me very close, and kissed me tenderly when we parted.

'Remember, dearest, Nellie has not long to live,' he whispered. 'And remember, too, that nothing, nothing, can now stand in the way of our marriage.'

For a long time after he had gone, I sat staring into the fire, thinking. My mind was a mass of confused thoughts, of disbelief, bewilderment, and angry grief. I had been betrayed by everyone, it seemed to me.

Those terrible years in prison, which could never be erased from my memory — how could Nellie have let me endure them?

At last, exhausted by the emotions of the evening, I went to bed, and strange, how despite everything, as usual, I missed Nellie's helping hand when I retired. Even though I had spent years without it, I had soon got back into the habit of her helping me off with my clothes, and brushing my hair.

When I sank into bed, I seemed to see her face all round me in the darkness. Was she lying awake too — perhaps suffering not only mentally, but physically? I relived the years of my motherless childhood as I lay there, remembering the tender, unselfish love which Nellie had lavished on me.

And for me, on an impulse, she had committed a crime against a man she knew I was unhappy with. If I had not fallen asleep that afternoon — if she had not seen tears on my cheeks — if — if — if . . .

So my thoughts ran on, and there was no answer; no comfort. To give me my 'freedom', Nellie had murdered a man, and seen me go to prison for it. I had suffered, and she had seen my suffering, and yet remained silent.

20

The following morning I rose early, after a night during which I had slept badly. Already, Liza had a cheerful fire burning. The outlook through the window was dreary indeed; a cold, misty drizzle was descending on the quiet street.

'Good day, ma'am. I suppose Miss Blacklock is no better?' Liza appeared with the breakfast tray.

'I'm afraid not.'

'But you are well now? You look a little pale, if I may say so.'

'I am quite well, now, thank you, Liza.'

I felt more composed. In fact, I felt almost detached, as though a good deal of feeling had been numbed. Up till the night before, on top of my concern for Nellie, was always the feeling that Charles would be going away to investigate Basil's death.

Well, he would not have to now. As he had said the night before, we could get married. Yes, I was truly free — free to marry him any time. But oh, the price I had paid for that freedom!

When Charles arrived, there was an unspoken question in his eyes. He came into the room, and clasped my hands in his.

'Dearest, I have been wondering how you were. It is cold and damp outside — '

'I do not expect to be going out today,' I said.

'Well, perhaps it is better not — '

There was a tap at the door, and Liza announced Mrs Tripp.

Charles and I were both surprised; surprise too showed clearly on the face of my visitor, at seeing Charles there in the morning.

'I trust I have not intruded,' said Mrs Tripp, after the preliminary greetings. 'We have seen little of you since your companion has been ill. I called round

325

to see how you were, Miss Hagan
— well, to see how Miss Blacklock is,
too.'

'There is no hope at all,' I said
quietly.

'Indeed? I am very sorry to hear that.
You know Edgar had to go to London
on business — ' she broke off.

'Yes, I did know, Mrs Tripp,' I said.

She seemed to be scrutinizing both
Charles and me in a very odd manner.
Why should she call unexpectedly on a
bleak winter morning, apart from the
fact that she would expect me to be
alone? She sat down in a proffered
chair, and Charles poked the fire, and
brought forth a brighter blaze.

'It was very kind of you to call on a
morning like this,' I said. For a moment
my visitor hesitated, and then she seemed
to make up her mind about something.

'As a matter of fact, Miss Hagan,
although I intended to call and see how
you were in any case, I have heard some
rather disturbing, well, I think it can
only be described as *gossip*.'

'Indeed,' said Charles quickly, looking up from the fire. 'I cannot imagine that you would be interested in listening to gossip, Mrs Tripp, much less repeating it.'

'No . . . well, you would be quite right in most cases. But this is something of a more serious nature.'

Suddenly I could feel my face growing hot, and the blood began to pound in my head. I was quite unable to speak.

'You had better say what it is, then,' said Charles coolly. 'If it concerns Miss Hagan, then it concerns me.'

'Well, some friends of ours — you met them briefly one evening — Mr and Mrs Braithwaite — well, I scarcely know how to tell you — '

'I believe I remember them very faintly from my childhood,' said Charles. 'Pray go on.'

'Yes — well — Mrs Braithwaite said she thought she knew not only you, Mr Ancroft, but Miss Hagan as well. Or rather, knew *of* her. She only confided this in me the other day, before they left for the north. I said you came from Ireland, but she said a young girl of that name had married the man who had bought Mr Ancroft's home — Battle Tower — I believe she called it — bought it from his brother — and — er — this girl had been widowed after a few months — '

'Yes?' Charles had gone pale, but he was quite composed. I found my voice then, although it didn't seem like me speaking at all.

'And that she had been charged with murdering her husband?' I said. 'Go on, say it, Mrs Tripp.'

'Well . . . er . . . yes.'

'And that it was brought in as criminal negligence, and she went to prison — and now she is out? And I am she? Is this the gossip you were bringing?'

Mrs Tripp coloured up. I had taken the wind out of her sails completely.

'Then . . . there is something in it?' she asked, speaking with obvious embarrassment.

'It is true that I have been to prison,' I said.

'Yes, that part is true,' interposed Charles. 'Maura's husband died from an overdose of laudanum, which was administered by her companion, Miss Blacklock. I intended to re-open inquiries concerning Mr Webber's death, but it will not be necessary now. I have a statement by Miss Blacklock with me, as it happens, signed and witnessed. Well, I suppose it was inevitable that the past would catch up with Maura. It's just coincidence that you should call this morning, because only yesterday, Miss Blacklock confessed that she had done it.'

He produced a piece of notepaper from his pocket, and handed it to my visitor. I had not yet read it myself — for what did a scrap of paper matter against the enormity of what had been done to me? However, I watched Mrs Tripp reading it, her face still very flushed.

'I see. I'm so sorry about this,' she

said slowly, putting it on the table beside her. 'There were, well, reasons why I thought it important to tell you what I had heard, Miss Hagan. It was not that I had any wish to pry — it seemed a serious matter to me. Of course, if you wish to pose as a single lady instead of a widow, that is your affair. But if Miss Blacklock has only just confessed to this crime herself, you must be in rather a shocked state.'

'I am in a very shocked state,' I said. I saw her glance at the mantelpiece. There was a letter from Edgar propped up beside the clock.

It was a pleasant, friendly letter, which I had received two days before and had not yet replied to. I felt she would have preferred Charles not to have been there. Undoubtedly, she knew her son was interested in me, and she had followed up Mrs Braithwaite's story immediately, because of this. She knew, too, that Charles had a powerful attraction for her daughter. She rose, and looked from me to him. For once, I think, her composure was shaken. She was quite nonplussed by the turn of events.

'Stay and have a drink of chocolate,' I said. 'You must not go so soon, Mrs Tripp. I have heard from Edgar, and he is well.' She smiled at that, and looked a bit more composed. I rang the bell for Liza.

'Philippa has been hunting this week,' said Mrs Tripp, changing the subject, as she seated herself again. 'You know she would like you both to join her. But of course, this illness of Miss Blacklock's — '

'We do not expect that to last much longer,' said Charles.

'You are indeed going through a sad time,' said Mrs Tripp, addressing me.

'That has been true of my life for many years,' I said. Liza arrived with the hot chocolate a few minutes later.

'I hope to put an end to Maura's sadness as soon as possible,' said Charles, while we were drinking it.

Mrs Tripp said nothing. She merely

looked at him enquiringly.

'As you know so much, you may as well know that Maura and I will be getting married as soon as possible. The barrier which stood in the way of Maura marrying me, or indeed anyone, has gone now. She has been imprisoned for a crime she never committed. We knew and loved each other a long time ago, Mrs Tripp.'

'Oh . . . indeed,' our visitor managed to say, plainly shaken to her very foundations. She was certainly flustered; whether she was relieved or not I was not sure.

'We thought it better under the circumstances to pose as distant cousins,' explained Charles blandly. 'I regret that we have had to practise deception in this matter, Mrs Tripp. It is a relief all round that it is no longer necessary.'

'It must indeed be,' she said, setting down her cup.

I had a feeling that by now she was eager to get away, and discuss Charles and me with her husband and Philippa, if nobody else. Neither of us asked her to keep it a secret; after all, what did it matter now? There was a bit more perfunctory conversation, and then Charles escorted her downstairs and to her waiting carriage.

'Well, Maura, all Bath will know about us soon,' he said when he came back into the room. He put his arms around me. 'You have nothing to hide now. You can prove your innocence to the world. You will come and see Nellie today?'

I shook my head.

'Don't ask me, Charles,' I said, and he wisely dropped the subject.

'We will plan our wedding, then, instead. And you had better write and tell Edgar Tripp the truth. It is only fair.'

He was right about that, and later I penned a letter, my feelings a curious mixture of bitterness, disbelief and sadness.

Even though I could now hold my head high, and marry the man I loved, I

333

felt none of the joy I should have done. Nellie's illness, Nellie's confession; my feelings of betrayal and outrage seemed to swamp even my love for Charles at that stage. Nevertheless, we arranged to have the banns called in the pretty church near Chippenham Crescent, and I decided to tell my kindly landlady the truth of the matter. She took this very well indeed. Naturally, I only gave her the very briefest outline of my past troubles, and she was quietly sympathetic.

'It is ending happily, Miss Hagan,' was her comment.

I then found myself surprisingly busy with preparations for our wedding. I never mentioned Nellie to Charles, although I knew that he still visited her. I tried to blot her out of my thoughts as much as possible.

There was a very good dressmaker in Bath, and I decided to have a blue costume made for my wedding. One afternoon I went for a fitting, accompanied by Charles, but when we returned to Chippenham Crescent, we had only been in the house half an hour before Liza ushered in Dr Rice.

'Good day, Miss Hagan,' he said abruptly. 'I have little time to spend talking, I'm afraid. I was summoned in hurriedly to Miss Blacklock. I was rather surprised to find you were not with her.'

He eyed me reprovingly, and went on — 'I advise you to go round immediately. I can do nothing further.'

I drew in my breath sharply. Despite my attempts to put Nellie out of my mind; despite my embittered grief, I had known this time would come, and would come very soon. But the shock was overpowering.

'Very well. Thank you, Dr Rice. We would have been seeing her later in any case. We will be at the nursing home straight away,' said Charles, putting a protective arm around me.

After the doctor had left, he drew me close to him.

'Maura, you *must* come. It is the end

— even now it may be too late. And she will die unforgiven — dearest, come for my sake, if nothing else.'

I wanted to protest, to refuse to accompany him, but the emotions which I was experiencing at that moment seemed to rob me of speech. Arm in arm we went out into the raw dusk of the afternoon. I sat huddled and trembling inside the carriage, and we set off at a good pace. I never spoke all the way to the nursing home. After a few attempts at conversation, Charles was silent too.

We were ushered into Nellie's room.

The curtains were drawn, a lamp was lit, and a good fire glowed in the hearth. We moved over to the bed, where the still, silent figure lay. Her eyes were closed.

'Nellie,' said Charles softly, 'Nellie, we've come to see you. It's Miss Maura.'

Her eyes remained closed. We sat on either side of the bed, and waited. The matron of the nursing home had said little, merely intimated that we could stay as long as we wished.

From her manner it was plain that she did not think it would be for long. It was hard to tell if Nellie was conscious or not. After the first shock of seeing her, the familiar feeling of numbness gripped me again.

It seemed impossible that this was Nellie; so strong, so wise, as she had seemed to me throughout my childhood, and girlhood too.

Could this poor creature be Nellie, not strong and wise as I had thought, but just a misguided woman who followed a dangerous impulse out of love, and was too weak and cowardly to take the consequences?

And now she was dying . . .

What life had she had but caring for other people; what love had she had except mine, and the love she had lavished on me, however misguided the action it had led her to? A sob broke from me. Life was too cruel. Charles stood up, and came round my side of the the bed to comfort me.

Perhaps the sound of my grief roused Nellie; it was hard to tell at that late stage. I bent down and kissed her.

'Miss Maura — ' she whispered.

I clasped her hands in mine; those once capable hands, now cold and limp.

'I have forgiven you, Nellie. It is past,' I said, trying to control my voice.

For a moment a flicker of understanding crossed her face. She half smiled.

'I've forgiven you,' I repeated.

'Mr Ancroft,' she whispered hoarsely. He bent down, and her weak hand reached for his, and folded it in mine.

'You will be happy, my lamb,' were her last words.

21

Charles and I sat in the drawing room of our house in Bath. A cheerful fire burnt in the hearth; every so often I leaned forward and held my hand in front of the dancing flames. Then, with my warm hand I would enfold a tiny pair of feet, and feel them curling faintly at the touch.

I smiled across at my husband. We had been married for over a year now, and our son, John Charles, was several weeks old. I bent and kissed his cherished head, with its soft down of brown hair. He was so like Charles; already the cleft in his chin was quite visible.

He was strong and healthy, too, unlike our first poor little son, born when I was in prison. But the bitterness and sadness of those memories had faded now; I felt that our happiness was complete.

Being married to Charles, not just in the sight of God, but in the eyes of the world, had given me the joy and security which I had never thought could be mine. In the soft glow of the lamplight the room was filled with peace and love, although it was a cold winter afternoon, and fast growing dark outside.

Charles knelt down on the hearthrug, and put his finger in John's hand.

'I think he's getting to look more like you now, Maura.'

'No,' I said. 'I think he looks like you. He looks like an Ancroft.'

Charles seemed rather thoughtful when I said that. And happy though we were with our son, it occurred to me that he had often looked thoughtful since he had become a father.

There was nothing for him to worry about, though; I was well, and so was the child. We had a very good nurse for him, and he was thriving. This was the time of day I liked best, when the baby was brought to us in the drawing room, and the three of us were together.

'Play a lullaby, dearest,' I said.

'They don't send him to sleep. You're the one who goes to sleep.'

'Oh, well, that was only once,' I said, smiling. 'You know I like you to play for me.'

He sat down at the piano, and ran his fingers across the keyboard. Then he began to play, but it was not a lullaby. It was a sad, haunting air which I did not know. And yet, I had the feeling I had heard it before. I had heard it somewhere, a long time ago. Memory stirred inside me, and tried to place it.

'What are you playing?' I asked.

'You don't know it?'

'No.'

'Are you sure?' He lifted his fingers from the keys and looked at me. And I knew by the expression on his face that there was something on his mind, and he was not entirely happy. He played the tune again, and this time he sang:

'I cannot get to my love, if I would dee, the water of the Tyne runs between him and me, and here I must stand

341

when the tear in my e'e, both sighing and sickly my sweetheart to see . . . '

He sang it right through.

'What is it? I don't know it,' I said lightly, but somehow I felt uneasy.

'It's an old Northumbrian folksong called The Water of The Tyne. My nurse used to sing it to me.'

Yes, I had heard that tune before. When I had lived in the Border country. I had heard it either played or sung.

The Water of The Tyne . . . why was he playing it now, though? He rose from the piano and came and sat close to me.

'Maura,' he said, 'we can't go on living here. I know you like it, and are happy. I wanted you to have time to get over Nellie's death, and, naturally, during the months before John was born, I wanted you to be tranquil. But now we have our son, and you are well. I've been doing a lot of thinking about the future.'

Somehow I knew what he was going to say next.

'I understand that it won't be easy for

342

you to return and live at Battle Tower. But you will be returning as my wife now — and remember it is John's birthright to live there. You cannot take that away from him, darling. He is the rightful heir to Battle Tower — the rightful heir.'

An icy web of fear seemed to creep down my spine. Battle Tower! That grim, northerly fortress, where I had suffered so grievously. I remembered the first time I had passed through that great oaken door, and seen the family motto, and beneath it the two words: *Justus Heres*. I remembered, too, Charles telling me about the old curse which fell upon any man, be he English or Scot, who took Battle Tower away from an Ancroft.

I pressed my baby close to me. He was my son, but the ancient blood of the warrior Ancrofts ran in his veins; the Ancrofts who had fought for their heritage so fiercely.

'I was born at Battle Tower,' went on Charles. 'I have never lost the feeling that it is my home. Darling, I know it calls for a great deal of courage from you to go back there after what has happened, but we have our child to think of. Maura, if you knew what it means to me — to go back there with you and my son! To live again at Battle Tower, where Ancrofts have lived for generations — '

He broke off, too overcome to continue.

I thought then of how his love for me had been tested. And it had stood the test. If I said no — if I refused to go back there, I knew that Charles would never be really happy. In his heart he might feel that I had failed him; that my love had not been strong enough to do this for him. And in a sense, the water of the Tyne might run between him and me all our married life . . .

'Please, for my sake, and for the sake of our son, forget the past, dearest. Think of the future — our future.'

Charles slipped his hand into mine, and suddenly, I was no longer afraid.

For his sake, and for the sake of our child — yes, I would return to Battle Tower.

'In the spring,' I said softly. 'We'll go back in the spring.'

'Thank you, darling,' whispered Charles. He kissed me, and I smiled at the happiness on his face.

I felt joy, too, because I was no longer afraid to return to that beautiful, rugged, lonely part of England, and to the impressive ancient home of the Ancrofts.

I wanted to show it all to John, when he was old enough. I wanted to show him where the Romans had camped long ago, and where Hadrian had built his great wall. I knew now that I could grow to love the Border country as much as Charles did. Slowly I would put down my roots in that land of sea-castles, of purple hills and solitary moorland.

My son would sit at his father's knee, and learn the history of the Ancrofts, and hear of the strife and warfare which once took place in the English Border-land. He would grow to manhood loving the wild sweep of the coastline, with the screaming gulls wheeling above the deserted beaches, while the cold German Ocean broke, foaming, over the rocks.

It was his inheritance. So too was Battle Tower, still standing proudly, still defying any man to take it from an Ancroft.

It was there waiting for us; waiting for the rightful heir to come home.

'In the spring, then, Maura,' said my husband.

Yes, we would return in the spring. The sun would be shining, although the Cheviots would still be snow-capped, lowering in the distance. And above them, as always, would be the unchanging blue of the windswept, Northumbrian sky.

THE END

We do hope that you have enjoyed reading this large print book.

Did you know that all of our titles are available for purchase?

We publish a wide range of high quality large print books including:
Romances, Mysteries, Classics
General Fiction
Non Fiction and Westerns

Special interest titles available in large print are:
The Little Oxford Dictionary
Music Book, Song Book
Hymn Book, Service Book

Also available from us courtesy of Oxford University Press:
Young Readers' Dictionary
(large print edition)
Young Readers' Thesaurus
(large print edition)

For further information or a free brochure, please contact us at:
Ulverscroft Large Print Books Ltd.,
The Green, Bradgate Road, Anstey,
Leicester, LE7 7FU, England.
Tel: (00 44) 0116 236 4325
Fax: (00 44) 0116 234 0205

THE FAMILY AT FARRSHORE

Kate Blackadder

After breaking up with Daniel, archaeologist Cathryn Fenton quite happily travels to Farrshore in Scotland to work on a major dig. In the driving rain, she gives a lift to Canadian Magnus Macaskill, then finds that they both lodge at the same place. The dig goes well, with Magnus filming the proceedings for a Viking series. But trouble looms in Farrshore — starting when Magnus learns that his son Tyler is coming over from Canada to be with his dad . . .

THE TEMP AND THE TYCOON

Liz Fielding

Talie Calhoun had briefly met billion-aire Jude Radcliffe whilst working as a temp at the Radcliffe Group. It was a rare holiday away from nursing her invalid mother. But when she's asked to accompany Mr Radcliffe to New York, she is over the moon. However, Radcliffe is furious with his secretary's choice of temp. But Talie is a vibrant woman and, as he becomes drawn to her, Jude becomes determined to take care of her and make her his own.

LOVE TRIUMPHANT

Margaret Mounsdon

Steve Baxter disappears while interior designer Lizzie Hilton is working on the refurbishment of his property. His brother, Todd, suspects Lizzie of becoming romantically involved with Steve, knowing that he is due to come into an inheritance upon marriage. Lizzie challenges Todd to find evidence to substantiate his outrageous allegation. But when Paul Owen appears on the scene Lizzie panics — because Paul can provide Todd with the evidence he is looking for . . .

FORGET-ME-NOT

Jasmina Svenne

As girls, Diana Aspley and Alice Simmonds swore that they would be friends forever. So Diana is devastated when she receives the news that Alice has died in unexplained circumstances. Then during her first London Season, she thinks she catches sight of a familiar figure from a carriage window . . . Diana is determined to get to the truth about Alice's fate, even if she has to persuade the aloof and eminently eligible Edgar Godolphin to help her.

RETURN TO BARRADALE

Carol MacLean

Melody has sworn never to return to Barradale, the island where she'd grown up — and been so unhappy . . . Now, living in Glasgow, she has forged a new life in the City for herself. But when the gorgeous Kieran Matthews turns up on her doorstep, demanding that she should go back with him to see her sick sister, she finds she cannot refuse. And for Melody, family secrets must be unravelled before Kieran's love can help to resolve her past.